DREA

Julia E. Clements

© Julia E. Clements 2017
Pink Quill Books
Cover by Francesco Valla

ISBN: 979-12-200-2261-3

Any images not created by the author are licensed under:
© CC0 Public Domain
Free for commercial use
No attribution required

For my wonderful readers, Francesco, Jess, Abigail, Bronwyn, Jack and Alex

Thank you for believing in this world of magic and dreams

CONTENTS

Chapter One
The Birthday Present

Danny cried out in his sleep as he plummeted down through the dark, inky blackness towards a single point of light that grew steadily brighter as he got closer. Suddenly he plunged out of the shadows into dazzling sunlight and saw that he was standing next to the old, gnarled oak at the bottom of the garden. In its sturdy branches above him was the tree house his dad had made so carefully two summers before.

He looked up at the familiar wooden chalet with its slanting roof, fake chimney and trap door entrance, remembering how his dad had warned him not to light any fires, joking that the fire brigade was busy enough as it was. A thick rope hung down from the tree house, swinging gently to and fro in a non-existent breeze, inviting him to climb up. He didn't want to go; the nightmare always began this way, appearing to be like any normal dream, and then rapidly turning into panic-filled horror. But, just like every other time, he had no choice.

He moved automatically towards the rope and began to climb the tree, using some pieces of wood that had been nailed into the trunk as foot holds. As he climbed he passed the sign he had written himself

7

in bright red paint: "*The Snug, Oak Tree Top, Garden's End, Rootling*" and the empty post box nailed below it. He glanced down and quickly wished he hadn't; the tree trunk seemed to be rushing away from the ground at an astonishing rate, the garden no longer visible through the swirling clouds below him. He grasped onto the rope, his head spinning, and determinedly carried on climbing. Finally, gasping for breath, he reached the trap door, pushed it open with one hand and hauled himself up into his tree house.

All of his things were where he had left them and nothing was out of place, yet he felt oddly uneasy, as if someone or something had been there recently. He stepped into the middle of the room that had been built around the tree trunk and sneezed as he brushed into some long, grey cobwebs dangling down from the ceiling. Disgusted, he frantically slapped his face to get rid of the sticky strands that had wrapped themselves around his head.

He realised that everything was very quiet, too quiet. There was not a single sound, no birds singing, no insects buzzing and droning in the branches of the oak. He tiptoed over to a window and looked out - there in the distance was the enormous, menacing black cloud, moving swiftly across the sky as usual. Suddenly the bright day turned dark as the cloud passed in front of the sun. Danny held his breath in trepidation, his heart thumping. He could hear the rope outside creaking as if someone was climbing up it, towards the open trap door in the floor. He hoped that this time it was his dad, coming to take him back to the house for his tea, even though he knew it was impossible, that his dad would never again come through the trap door.

A scream built up in his throat as a dark, shadowy figure glided into the tree house and slowly turned around. Two piercing red eyes glowered at him, as bright as burning coals. The spectre glided towards Danny, its long, black cloak swishing around its feet. Terrified, he stumbled backwards until he could feel the wooden wall of the chalet behind him and he had nowhere left to run. This was the point where he usually woke up, the spectre melting away as he sat up in bed with his eyes wide open in fright. But this time it was different. This time the spectre continued to advance, until he could see the vapour from its fetid breath just a few inches from his face. His frightened scream reverberated around the tree house as a long, skeletal hand reached out and slowly beckoned to him. At the same time an enormous, swirling vortex of air appeared above the trapdoor, spinning violently. The tree house started to disintegrate and Danny grabbed onto the trunk, dodging pieces of wooden planks while desperately trying to save himself from falling into the roaring whirlwind, his books and toys flying past him. Air whistled past his ears and his arms ached from grasping so tightly onto the trunk. As his grip slowly loosened and his fingertips slipped on the rough bark, he could feel his body being pulled towards the vortex. Unable to hold on any longer, he suddenly let go and hurtled through the air towards the raging maelstrom and the terrifying apparition waiting for him...

Danny woke up with a start, his heart pounding furiously. Reaching over, he switched on the light on his bedside table, relieved as its golden glow drove away the last wisps of the nightmare from his mind. He lay back in bed, trying not to remember the dream, but parts of it kept slithering back into his head like a grotesque serpent trying to sink its poisonous fangs into him.

He screwed his eyes tight shut, struggling to banish the terrifying images but it only seemed to make things worse; he could still see the two glowing red eyes, trying to force him to remember the nightmare, to start reliving it all over again. He opened his eyes again and lay still, his body trembling as he tried hard not to cry. The nightmare had begun about a year earlier, soon after his dad had died, although this was the first time it had ended in such a frightening way.

Danny glanced over at his clock and groaned when he saw that it was only four in the morning. He would have to try to go back to sleep, otherwise he would be too tired for his birthday party later that day. He had wanted to have his party in his beloved tree house but his mum had said no, she was scared that it would collapse with twenty children thundering around inside it. He turned the light off, pulled the bed-covers up over his head and hardly had time to wonder how long it would take him to drop off before he was in a deep, dreamless sleep.

Danny changed into his pyjamas, chattering excitedly to his mum. "That was the coolest birthday ever, Mum! The chemistry kit Mike gave me is brilliant, and that construction set is fantastic, and all those new books to read. Dad would have loved it..." His voice trailed off and he busied himself sorting through the pile of presents.

A pained look came over his mum's face but she smiled at him. "You can talk about him, you know Danny," she said, brushing his hair out of his eyes.

"It's OK," he mumbled, picking birthday cards up off the floor. She didn't insist but helped him put everything away, listening patiently to his chatter.

"It was a great party, Mum, thanks," he continued brightly, trying to cover up how sad he felt. He took a deep breath and tried again. "Everyone said they liked the dinosaur theme, it was really cool!"

"Did you see their faces when I brought your birthday cake out?" his mum laughed. "Aunty Lisa did a really good job of copying that T-Rex out of your book, it looked very life-like!"

"Yeah, Sarah's little sister hid behind her mum... she said that she could see blood on its teeth!" Danny replied, relieved that he had steered his mum away from talking about his dad.

"So that's why she didn't want to eat any," she said. "Didn't put *you* off, though, did it?"

"I ate three pieces," Danny said proudly. "I do feel a bit full up now." He pulled up his pyjama top and examined his stomach.

11

"Looks like you've eaten a whole T-Rex!" his mum exclaimed. She poked his tummy. "I can still hear it growling in there!"

"*Mum!*" Danny giggled. He rolled around on the floor, laughing loudly as his mum relentlessly tickled him until he begged for mercy.

"OK, Danny," she said, finally letting him go. "It's time you went to bed, it's getting late. It's been a long day."

Danny nodded, not very enthusiastically. He wished the day would never end, it had been a lot of fun. He climbed into bed, yawning. His mum tucked the sheets around him, her long, dark hair falling over her face. She pushed it back with her hands and winked at Danny, her eyes twinkling.

"I've got one last present for you," she whispered. Danny's eyes suddenly opened wide, all thoughts of sleep forgotten.

"Another one!" he gasped.

"Yes, and it's very special. I've been saving it for your tenth birthday, when you would be old enough to understand just how special it is."

"How special what is, Mum?"

"Oh, you'll see." She reached into her pocket and pulled out an envelope. She looked at it for a moment, then handed it to Danny. "Open it."

He held the envelope in his hand, turning it around. It was plain and white, it didn't *seem* very special, but from the expression on his mum's face he could tell it was very important. He slowly pulled the edges of the envelope apart, not wanting to open it too quickly, imagining that there was something magical inside. When the envelope was open, he put in his hand and pulled out… a piece of shiny silver paper, folded in half. He held it in his hand and looked up at his mum.

"Read it, Danny," she urged, smiling encouragingly at him.

He unfolded it. On the inside there was written, in thick black letters:

ONE RETURN TICKET TO DREAMLAND

Underneath, in smaller letters, was written:

INSTRUCTIONS: PLACE UNDER PILLOW BEFORE GOING TO SLEEP
VALIDITY: FOR AS LONG AS THE HOLDER BELIEVES

Danny looked up at his mum. "Is this a joke?" he asked, a bit hurt.

"Why do you say that?"

"Well, you know… a trip to Dreamland… sounds like something you'd give to a baby to make them go to bed!"

His mum laughed. "Oh, it's nothing like that. Believe me, this is real. It used to belong to me." She closed her eyes for a moment and images flashed through her mind of long-lost friends and exciting adventures enjoyed many years before. She sighed deeply, then caught sight of the unconvinced look on Danny's face.

"But if you don't believe me," she said, smiling as Danny shook his head, "why don't you try leaving it under your pillow tonight and see what happens?"

Danny decided to go along with the joke. "OK, I'll give it a try. Can I just ask you one thing, though?"

"What?"

"Why are you giving it to me? If it's so wonderful, why don't *you* use it?"

"Because, Danny, I grew up," she replied sadly. She leaned over and ruffled his blond hair, kissing him on his forehead. "Goodnight, Danny, no reading tonight. Close your eyes and go and have fun in Dreamland."

As she softly closed the door Danny lay back in his bed, looking at the ticket in his hand, then he glanced over at the paperback on his bedside table. His mum had said to go straight to sleep, even though he would have liked to read for a while. He loved books, he would read anything and everything. He loved to drift away into imaginary worlds, becoming friends with the characters in the stories and living their adventures with them. He often read by torchlight under his blanket, unable to put the book down until he had finished it, even though he hated that empty feeling he got when the story was over and the characters were gone.

Danny's mum adored reading books too. Every Friday night they would curl up in her bed and read together, creating weird voices for all the different people in the tale. Danny had never told her how sad it made him to arrive at the end of a book, but somehow she knew anyway and would encourage him to continue with the story, inventing new adventures for all the characters he'd met whilst reading. He couldn't ever imagine a time when books weren't the most important thing in his life.

He glared at the ticket, then shoved it under his pillow. He could hear his mum moving about downstairs and the TV murmuring quietly. He felt his eyes slowly getting heavier, until he could no longer keep them open.

A little while later, Danny felt as if he were falling. He opened his eyes and saw a grey mist swirling around him. This time he didn't feel scared, like he usually did during the nightmare, even though he sensed that he was plummeting down at a great speed. Straining his eyes, he could just make out objects hurtling through the nothingness close by him: enormous lollipops and sticks of candy, toy soldiers, roller coasters, merry-go-rounds and dozens of toy woolly mammoths. They spun ever faster around him, becoming more and more confused until he felt quite dizzy, and then suddenly everything stopped abruptly. As his head gradually ceased spinning, he realised that he was finally standing on the ground.

It took a while for his eyes to get used to the brilliant sunlight, but as he slowly looked around his mouth dropped open in amazement. It seemed that he was in an enormous fairground that stretched as far as he could see in every direction. There were roundabouts with brightly coloured horses, candy floss stalls, dodgems, a shooting range, even a "win a goldfish" stall, and there were crowds of people everywhere. Relaxed parents watched their children having fun on the dodgems, a group of sticky-faced boys walked around holding frothy pink sticks of candy floss, and young children screamed in delight on the merry-go-rounds. Everywhere music blasted out from hidden speakers on the rides, and above all the noise he could just about hear the numerous stall owners shouting out to attract customers, each one trying to be the loudest. The smell of doughnuts and freshly made popcorn filled the air, making his mouth water.

As he looked around, a small girl with a toffee apple grasped tightly in her hand ran past him towards a group of children, then suddenly disappeared into thin air. Danny blinked in surprise.

"Where am I?" he asked in bewilderment.

"Why, in Dreamland, of course!" a voice said next to him.

Danny jumped in fright; he hadn't realised that there was anyone nearby. He turned to ask more questions, but the words stuck in his throat. Next to him was the largest cricket he'd ever seen! Standing on its hind legs it was at least two metres tall, bright green in colour and with enormous, bulbous eyes that gazed unblinkingly at him. But even stranger was the fact that it was wearing a straw hat and a waistcoat, and had a walking stick hooked over one of its arms.

"Who… what?" Danny didn't know what to say, but he didn't want to offend the creature. With an effort he stammered, "D-Dreamland?"

"Yes," the cricket replied. "You must have been given a ticket."

Danny remembered the silver ticket his mum had given him and nodded. "I thought it was just a joke," he mumbled.

"As you can see, it was definitely no joke," the cricket said brightly. "My name's Argill, by the way. And you are…?"

"Oh, I'm Danny, Daniel Green," he replied hurriedly.

"And how old are you, Daniel Green?"

"I'm ten years old today," Danny said proudly.

"Of course. Ten. That's a good age. I'm two hundred and thirty-four."

"Wow," Danny said, impressed. "You're older than my gran!"

The cricket chuckled, and then became serious once more. "You see all this, Daniel?" he asked, pointing at the fairground with his walking stick. Danny nodded. "This all comes from your imagination. Everything has been created by you… well, almost everything… and you can change it as and when you want."

"*I* can change it?" Danny exclaimed.

"Certainly. This is your dream, anything can happen. As you fall through the grey mist, images appear from your subconscious and hey presto! When you arrive here, you're in the place you made with your imagination. Today it's a fairground, tomorrow it could be pirates in a ship on the open sea, or cowboys and indians, or cars racing across country… well, you get the idea."

"It's just like being in a story," Danny sighed. He looked around, curious. "So, where do I go? What can I do here?"

The cricket smiled at him. "You can go where you want and do what you like. But first, a word of warning."

"Uh oh," Danny said. Usually this meant that he wouldn't be allowed to do anything remotely exciting.

"This is *Dreamland*, Daniel. I'm sure that most of your dreams are wonderful, but you probably also have some frightening ones, don't you?"

Danny remembered the nightmare he'd had only the night before, where he had woken up trembling. He nodded. "But Dreamland can't be scary, can it?" he pleaded with Argill. "Look, everyone's having fun and they're all so happy."

"No, Dreamland isn't a scary place, Daniel. You are in charge of everything that happens here, and everyone you meet will be very friendly and will help you have exciting adventures. *But*," and here his face became very serious, "you must never go to the edge of Dreamland."

"The edge?" Danny repeated, starting to feel confused. "Dreamland has an edge?"

"All around Dreamland lies the Dark Forest. This is the scary part of Dreamland, the nightmare area, if you like. It separates your Dreamland from all the other children's Dreamlands." He looked at the incredulous expression on Danny's face and laughed. "Yes, Danny, other children have silver tickets under their pillows and visit Dreamland every night. It would be very difficult for every one of you to create your own world if there was only one Dreamland!"

Danny thought for a moment, then nodded. "Yes, I can understand that. But can't I go and visit the other children's worlds?"

Argill shook his head. "It would be dangerous if everyone could pass from world to world whenever they wanted… you would remain trapped in another child's Dreamland when he or she woke up. Therefore the Dark Forest stretches for miles in all directions to prevent you from entering the other Dreamlands. Only the unicorns know the way through and even they are wary of travelling too far in. You see, other creatures live there… trolls, giants, ogres, all the monsters from the fairy tales."

Danny gulped. He began to realize why his mum had given him the ticket only now – it definitely wasn't a place for babies!

"And Stregona lives there," Argill continued.

"S-Stregona?" Danny murmured.

"She is an evil witch who reigns over all the malevolent creatures in the forest. She hates children and will do anything to get rid of you."

"Oh."

"Anyway, as long as you don't go near the forest, you've got nothing to worry about. Dreamland is a fantastic place, and you will have lots of wonderful adventures."

"What happens to Dreamland when I wake up?" Danny asked.

"It fades into nothingness and becomes the grey mist you travelled through to get here," Argill replied.

"And you? And all the other people here?" Danny cried.

"I will be here every time you return," Argill promised. "I'm here to help you when you need me. As for all these other people? Some will come back, while some will go off to other Dreamlands, like the little girl with the toffee apple you saw earlier. But any friends you make here will be waiting for you when you return."

"Good," Danny said, relieved.

"Well, I think it's about time you went to explore your Dreamland, Daniel. If I were you, I'd try that stall over there." Argill pointed to a brightly painted stall with a sign saying: SCORE 300 WITH 5 BALLS AND WIN A WOOLLY MAMMOTH! Danny could see lots of toy woolly mammoths hanging all around the frame of the stall.

"Go and talk to Tom the gnome and tell him Argill sent you," the cricket suggested. He bowed down low, then turned and walked away. "Goodbye, young Daniel," he called back over his shoulder.

"Goodbye, Argill, and thank you." Suddenly Danny felt all alone. He began walking towards the stall, smiling as two boys ran by waving enormous lollipops in front of them. Suddenly one tripped and his lollipop flew through the air. He lay sprawled on the ground and burst into tears. Danny watched the lollipop as it soared into the sky and began falling back down again. Then he remembered Argill's words: *'You can change things as and when you want.'* He closed his eyes and concentrated on the sweet, willing it to stop falling. To his amazement it hung suspended in mid-air right in front of him. He stepped forward and took hold of it.

The boy stopped crying as Danny knelt beside him and handed him the lollipop. "Thanks," he mumbled, trying to wipe away his tears with his grubby hands and only succeeding in leaving black streaks all over his cheeks.

"My pleasure," Danny grinned. He stood up and straightened his shoulders, suddenly feeling on top of the world. "Right," he said to himself, "let's go and meet Tom the gnome."

Danny found himself standing in front of a small, stocky man wearing a pointed yellow hat, a green shirt, and yellow and green striped trousers. He had friendly, brown eyes, a large nose and a bushy beard that seemed to cover most of his face. Two sharply pointed ears were just visible beneath his wiry, black hair.

"Roll up, roll up, come and win a woolly mammoth," the little man yelled, his voice surprisingly loud. He saw Danny and winked at him. "Come on young man, give it a go. Try and score three hundred points with five balls or less!"

"I don't have any money," Danny said regretfully.

"You don't have any money? Who needs money here in Dreamland? Come on, have a go." The gnome placed five tennis balls on the counter.

"Where's the target?" Danny asked.

"There." The gnome pointed to an enormous red circle painted on a wooden board which was standing just a few feet away. There was the number 300 written in the middle of it.

"I have to hit *that*?" Danny laughed.

"I know it's difficult but try anyway," the gnome replied gravely.

Danny shrugged and threw the first ball.

"Three hundred points with one ball!" the gnome shouted excitedly. "I knew you were a winner as soon as I saw you. Here," and he handed Danny the largest toy mammoth he had. "Star prize," he explained.

Danny took the toy, laughing. "Are you Tom the gnome?" he asked, remembering Argill's advice.

"Yes I am. And you are?"

"I'm Danny. I was speaking with Argill the cricket and he said to speak with…"

"Danny? Danny! Well bless my soul, of course you are! Welcome to Dreamland, Danny," the little man said, shaking his hand vigorously. "It really is a pleasure to meet you," he beamed. Danny found himself liking the gnome immensely.

"This is my first trip. I don't really know what to do. Can you help me?"

"Help you?" Tom said. "Of course I can. I'll show you all around Dreamland, come on! Oh, just leave that here," he added, seeing Danny struggling to carry the enormous mammoth under his arm.

For the next hour or so, Tom took Danny all around the fairground, introducing him to everyone. After a while he gave up trying to remember all their names and just nodded politely to them all. Eventually they reached the last stall on the furthest edge of the fairground. While Tom was introducing him to the owner, "This is Stupendo, the greatest magician in all of Dreamland," Danny found himself gazing out at the dark mass of trees just a little way away. After having spoken with Stupendo and promised to go and see his magic show one evening, Danny turned to Tom.

"Is that the Dark Forest?" he asked excitedly, as they walked away.

"Yes, it is and no, we can't go there," replied Tom, glancing anxiously at Danny. "Didn't Argill tell you not to go there?"

"Yes, he said monsters live there."

"He's quite right. No one enters the Dark Forest, it's very easy to get lost."

"But Argill said that the unicorns know the way," Danny said.

"He must have also told you that even the unicorns don't go too far in," Tom said sternly.

"So the unicorns must live near the edge?" Danny asked innocently.

"Well, they live in large groups not too far inside the forest."

23

"I would *love* to see a unicorn," Danny sighed. "If we only went a little way in, perhaps we could see one."

Tom realised that he had been tricked. "This is your world Danny, I can only warn you not to go in. However, if you really want to go, I can't stop you."

Danny grinned in triumph. Then he shivered as he looked again at the Dark Forest. It seemed very menacing and forbidding.

"Well, if you're sure about this, let's go," Tom said.

"You're coming too?" Danny was relieved that he didn't have to go in there alone.

"I've been in the forest once or twice, looking for mushrooms," Tom said. "We should be all right if we don't go too far in. Ready?"

Danny nodded. They set off towards the nearby trees.

"Wait!" a voice cried from behind them. "Wait, Tom!"

Danny and Tom both turned to see a girl running towards them, her long copper hair streaming out behind her and her summer dress flapping around her long legs. She caught up with them, panting heavily.

"P-Peaches s-said that you were showing D-Danny around," she said, trying to catch her breath. "I can't believe you didn't bring him to Mum and Dad's stall, Tom." She looked accusingly at the gnome, who blushed.

"I'm sorry, Lucy. I was going to come to you next, honest."

"That's OK, Tom," she said, laughing. "I'm here now, you can introduce us."

"Of course. Danny, this is Lucy Connors, her parents run the sweet stall. Lucy, this is Danny."

"How do you do?" she said, solemnly shaking Danny's hand, a twinkle in her startling blue eyes. Her face was covered in freckles and her cheeks dimpled when she smiled. Danny thought she looked like she'd be a lot of fun.

"Pleased to meet you," he said. "A sweet stall, huh? Cool. You should have taken me there right away, Tom," he added, frowning at the gnome. He grinned as Tom began stuttering an apology. "I'm sure you would have taken me there eventually," he said sternly, trying not to laugh. "So, where are you going?" Lucy asked, walking between Danny and Tom.

"*Danny* wants to see some unicorns, so we're going into the Dark Forest," Tom answered quickly, glaring at Danny.

"Into the forest? Are you crazy? Danny, you mustn't go in there," Lucy cried, pulling on both their arms.

"It's OK, Lucy, we're not going very far in," Danny said. "And Tom says he's been there before. We'll be all right," he added, trying to convince himself as much as Lucy.

She shook her head. "Don't be so stupid! Haven't you been told not to go there? I can't believe you agreed to take him, Tom, it's dangerous!"

Tom's face flushed. "I *did* tell him not to go, but he wouldn't listen," he said angrily. "*You* try telling him." An argument broke out between Tom and Lucy, each trying to shout above the other to be heard. Just when it seemed as if they would come to blows, a noise made Lucy turn around. She stared at the trees in front of them, her hand over her mouth. Tom also stopped shouting, and he and Danny looked in the same direction.

Walking beneath the trees was the most magnificent unicorn, its flowing white mane gracefully rising and falling with each step it took. The sun reflected brightly off its pure white coat and they found that it was painful to look at it for too long. Danny felt as if his heart would stop beating as he watched the creature emerge from the forest, its head held low to avoid knocking into the branches of the trees with its magnificent, long, ivory-coloured horn.

Chapter Two
In The Dark Forest

Nobody spoke as the unicorn moved towards them. Danny gazed in amazement at the wonderful creature, hardly daring to breathe. The unicorn stopped before him and bowed its head slightly, its mane rippling along its neck in glossy waves. Danny saw that silver tears glistened under its eyes.

"My name is Argenta, Queen of the unicorns," she said, her voice conjuring up images of a clear mountain stream running over tiny pebbles. "You are Danny?"

Danny nodded, too overwhelmed to speak. He didn't trust his voice not to tremble, so he remained silent.

"I need your help," the unicorn said quietly. "And your friends', too," she added, gazing at Tom and Lucy.

Danny finally found his voice. "Oh, of course," he stammered. "Er, this is Lucy and this is Tom."

"Hello," Argenta said. Lucy and Tom stuttered a reply; they were both just as overcome with awe as Danny. The unicorns rarely ventured out of the Dark Forest and neither of them had been this close to one before.

"Why do you need my help?" Danny asked in an unnaturally high voice, after a couple of minutes of uncomfortable silence during which he tried to pluck up the courage to speak. Argenta shook her head and two silver tears dropped slowly to the ground where they shattered into a million tiny droplets.

"Our herd was grazing in a clearing at sunset yesterday when a giant suddenly attacked us with an enormous wooden club. He hit several unicorns, including Fleetfoot, my husband, before we had time to react. Luckily no one was badly hurt, but in the confusion my son Joey and I became separated from the others. We ran into the forest to escape but the giant followed us and… and…" she gave an enormous sob, "caught us and carried Joey away with him before I could stop him."

There was a stunned silence. "A giant stole your son?" Tom roared. "But giants never attack unicorns, they have too much respect for them!"

"That is how it has always been, ever since our ancestors first came to the Dark Forest," Argenta replied. "I cannot understand why this one attacked us and took my son."

Danny looked at her. "What can I do?" he asked, a little nervously.

"Find Joey for me," Argenta answered.

"In there?" Danny pointed at the forest.

"Yes, the giant is in the forest," Argenta said patiently. "Will you help me?"

"I'm sorry, but why don't the unicorns search for your son? Why ask Danny to do it?" Lucy blurted out.

"Because most of my herd escaped deep into the Dark Forest and it will take days for them to return to me, and because the giant has blocked the way, child, and I cannot follow him," Argenta replied. "When I heard that Danny had arrived, I knew that if anyone can persuade the giant to release Joey, he can." She looked again at Danny, waiting for his answer.

All of a sudden, his face lit up. "But I can change things. I can make the giant give Joey back to you just by imagining it."

"I am sorry, Danny," Argenta replied sadly. "You can control events in your Dreamland but the Dark Forest has not been created by you, therefore you cannot change anything in there. You must go in."

Danny nodded, trying to look more confident than he felt. "I'll go," he said determinedly. "You two don't have to come," he added, as Lucy and Tom gaped at him.

"Of course we'll come!" they both cried.

Argenta looked at them, her eyes filled with gratitude. "I can show you where the giant took Joey," she said, turning away from them. The three friends slowly followed her into the Dark Forest.

It took Danny's eyes a while to adjust to the gloom under the trees after the bright sunshine outside. He grunted as he hit his head yet again on a low branch. He could make out the gleam of Argenta's white body in front of him, not even the dark shadows could dim the brightness of her coat. Time ceased to exist as they walked through the darkness together, holding hands so that they wouldn't get lost. Argenta led them along hidden paths further into the forest.

"I hope she knows where she's going," Tom muttered, trying to turn his comment into a cough as Argenta snorted angrily.

Finally, after what seemed like ages, they arrived in a clearing where the sun's rays managed to filter down through the trees. Argenta turned to them, their faces pale in the half-light.

"The giant attacked us here," she whispered angrily.

Lucy looked around nervously, half expecting the giant to come crashing through the trees at any moment.

"When my herd scattered, Joey and I ran in that direction." She pointed with her horn. "He followed us and cornered us a bit further on. Come, I'll show you."

They walked down a narrow track until Argenta stopped. Several enormous tree trunks lay end to end across their path. "He had obviously prepared this trap," she said. "We ran up to this point and when we tried to turn, it was too late… he was right behind us. He picked Joey up, jumped over the trees and was gone. I tried to follow him but I couldn't find a way around the barrier at all."

Danny looked at the tree right in front of them. He could just make out the top of the trunk in the shadows, a metre or so above his head. "We have to climb over this?" he asked.

"It is impossible to go around it, the giant has blocked it at either end," Argenta replied.

Tom cleared his throat. "We want to help you, ma'am," he said, "but once we're over the tree, how will we find our way to the giant? We can hardly see in this darkness, and we don't know the paths like you do."

"I have already thought of that," Argenta said. "I have asked my friend Lucinda if she will help you. She should be here at any moment."

Danny, Lucy, and Tom looked around, but couldn't see anyone nearby. Then Lucy saw a light in the distance, moving towards them.

"There!" she shouted.

As Danny and Tom looked, the light slowly grew bigger until it came to a halt just before them, hanging in mid-air. Danny gasped; it wasn't a light but a fairy, about 20 centimetres tall. She shimmered like a star in the night sky, her silver hair floating gently around her elfin face. She hovered before him, giggling mischievously.

"Hi Danny," she laughed in a tinkling voice. "I promised Argenta I'd show you the way through the forest."

"Do you know where the giant is?" Danny said hopefully.

"No, afraid not. But he should be easy enough to find. A big oaf like him crashing through the forest should leave a pretty clear path for us to follow!"

"How do we get over the tree?" Lucy asked.

"You can stand on my back," Argenta said. "You should be able to reach the top that way."

Lucinda darted excitedly about as the three friends, one by one, struggled to climb the trunk. Eventually, after a lot of effort, all three were sitting on top of the tree, nursing skinned knees and grazed palms.

"And now, how do we get down?" Tom groaned, trying to see how far the ground was beneath them. Lucinda giggled. As they were trying to figure out how to get down from the trunk, she flew behind each one and gave them an enormous push.

"Ooomph!"

"Aaaargh!"

"Urg!"

Tom, Danny and Lucy suddenly found themselves in a muddled heap on the ground, a surprised look on their faces.

"Well, you did ask," Lucinda chuckled. "That was the quickest way I could think of!"

Grumbling, the three friends picked themselves up, checking for broken bones. Then they set off down the path again, following Lucinda's light this time. There could be no doubt which direction the giant had gone in; there were twigs and branches strewn across the forest floor and many trees leaned at funny angles. After they had been walking for some time, Lucy stopped.

"What's that noise?" she said. The others strained to listen.

"I can't hear anything," Tom said.

"Shh!" Danny whispered. "I can hear something too. Let's be quiet."

They crept forward slowly, hardly daring to breathe. Now they could all hear something, a deep, rumbling noise further ahead. Lucinda dimmed her light and stayed close to Danny, a frightened look on her face.

"What is it?" she asked.

Danny shrugged his shoulders and motioned to her to go on. They arrived at another clearing which was even darker and gloomier than the rest of the forest. The branches of the trees stretched high overhead, densely packed together and blocking out all daylight. The noise was unbearably loud here, a deep rhythmic rumbling like thunder. They held hands and moved into the clearing. Lucinda remained behind, too scared to go with them.

Tom stopped suddenly as he crashed into something solid. "Ouch!" he exclaimed, rubbing his head.

"Lucinda," Danny called softly, "we need some light here."

The fairy reluctantly flew over and moved so that her light shone on the object. A huge, dirty wall rose up before them. Danny reached out and touched it. The wall felt leathery and smooth and it was covered in moss and lichen, making it too slippery to climb.

"Go up," Danny whispered to the fairy. She obediently flew up the wall until she reached the top. Tom, Danny and Lucy gasped in shock. At the top of the wall there were five enormous toes!

Danny suddenly realized what it was. "It's the giant's foot! He's lying down asleep here in the clearing!"

"That noise must be the giant snoring," Tom laughed. "All we need to do is find Joey and get away before the giant wakes up."

"I like your plan," Danny said. "Lucinda, will you light our way?" The fairy nodded and they set off around the giant's foot. Danny gazed up, amazed at how big it was. They walked quietly past the giant's ankle and up beside his leg, until after a while Danny bumped into something. He signalled to the others to stop and Lucinda flew over to him. Her light showed a thick rope stretching from the giant's hand to a small, white creature curled up on the floor fast asleep, its short horn resting on its flank.

"Joey!" Lucy whispered. They ran across to the baby unicorn, hardly believing their luck. The animal stirred as they reached it and looked up, blinking in Lucinda's light.

"Who are you?" he asked sleepily.

"I'm Danny and this is Tom and Lucy. Your mum, Argenta, asked us to find you, Joey."

"Wow, I'm being rescued!" he shouted in delight, jumping to his feet.

"*Ssshhh!*" the three friends said together, glancing nervously at the sleeping giant, who shifted slightly but carried on snoring.

"Be quiet," Danny ordered. "Lucinda, shine your light here please, so I can undo this knot."

After some time (Joey found it impossible to stay still for long and kept turning to see what was going on) Danny managed to undo the rope. The baby unicorn shook its head and began prancing around them, pleased to be free.

"Let's go," Lucy said anxiously, wanting to get far away from the giant.

"Good idea," Danny said. "Tom, Lucy, you go in front. Joey and I will be right behind you. Lucinda, you light the way."

They began creeping out of the clearing, Danny keeping a firm hold on Joey's mane. As they drew level with the giant's feet, Danny tripped over a fallen branch. He let go of Joey, who instantly started jumping around again.

"Joey, no!" Danny called, but it was too late. The unicorn slipped and crashed into the giant's foot, pricking it with his horn. The giant snorted and grunted, his hand groping instinctively for the rope, but didn't wake up.

Joey picked himself up and ran towards Danny, terrified. Lucy and Tom helped Danny carry the creature, trying to move as quietly as possible. They stumbled frequently, unable to see more than a few centimetres in front of them. Lucinda grabbed a fallen branch and muttered a few words in a strange language. The branch burst into flame, crackling loudly, as she handed it to Tom.

"At least you can see where you're going," she whispered. The three friends moved forward, but Joey began struggling again.

"Let… me… go!" he demanded and kicked his legs. Lucy and Tom dropped him and Danny fell over backwards. Joey jumped up, swishing his tail in excitement.

"Careful, Joey," Lucinda shouted. The unicorn's tail caught the torch Tom was holding and knocked it out of his hand. Sparks flew everywhere as it shot upwards and landed on the giant's foot. The smell of singed flesh filled the air. Nobody moved.

"AAARRRGGGHHH!" the giant roared, clambering awkwardly to his feet.

"Run!" Danny yelled. But before they could do anything, an enormous hand scooped them up into the air.

Danny, Tom, Lucy, Joey and Lucinda were standing in the middle of a wide, calloused hand, looking at the biggest face they had ever seen. The giant peered at them with two eyes as big as pizza plates set above a massive, potato-shaped nose. Huge tufts of bristly hair poked out from his nostrils, making up for the lack of hair on his head.

"WHO DARES TO WAKE GRULLO?" he bellowed.

They fell over from the blast of his breath. Joey teetered on the edge of the giant's hand, until Lucinda managed to pull him back to safety.

"Please, don't speak so loudly!" Danny shouted.

"Sorry," the giant said, his voice now a soft growl. He looked more closely at them, and noticed Joey.

"What? Are you trying to steal Grullo's unicorn?" he said angrily, his voice getting louder again.

"His mother asked me to rescue him," Danny replied, trying not to sound scared. "You stole him from her!"

The giant's mouth spread into an enormous grin. Danny thought that his teeth looked like huge tombstones placed haphazardly into his gums.

"And how do *you* think you'll get him from Grullo?" the giant demanded. "Grullo could swallow you all up in one mouthful. Crunch, crunch, CRUNCH!" His teeth clashed together with a horrible noise.

Danny swallowed nervously. "I was hoping you'd give Joey to me. His mother is very worried about him."

"*Give* him to you? The trolls wouldn't like that, no way. And then they wouldn't give Grullo his prize and Grullo wants his prize."

"Trolls?" Tom shouted. "What do trolls have to do with this?"

The giant sighed deeply. Danny grabbed hold of Lucinda as she flew past him, blown away by the giant's breath.

"Th-thanks," she gasped. "I wish he wouldn't do that!"

"The trolls make deal with Grullo," the giant said. "Grullo gets them little children and they give Grullo silver and gold treasure. Grullo clever... he steal cute baby unicorn so little children see it and follow it into the forest. Then Grullo catch children."

"Why do the trolls want children?" Danny asked.

The giant just stared at him without saying anything.

37

"Danny, the trolls feed on the grey mist which remains here when the children awake. The less a child sleeps, the more grey mist there is for them to eat," Lucy explained. "Sometimes, when they're desperate, the trolls venture into Dreamland to scare the children just so they wake up."

"So if Grullo uses Joey to lure children from all the different Dreamlands into the Dark Forest..." Danny began.

"The trolls will be waiting to scare the children and wake them up," Lucy finished for him.

"And Dreamland will just be a swirling grey mist," Tom added.

Joey stamped his hoof angrily. "I'll never agree to help you, *never*!" he exclaimed.

Grullo's lips began to tremble and giant teardrops fell from his eyes. "B-but you've g-got to h-help Grullo," he sobbed. "G-Grullo want the g-gold and s-silver treasure. Look!"

The giant lowered them to the ground, near a huge sack at the edge of the clearing. He opened it with trembling fingers, and spilled the contents onto a pile of dead leaves. They gasped as they saw a huge heap of shiny gold and silver coins.

"Grullo l-love shiny things and the trolls have lots of these," he said.

Danny moved closer to the mound of coins. "Lucy, come and see," he said a moment later. Lucy joined him, followed by Tom and a rather subdued Joey. Lucinda hovered overhead so that they could see by

38

her light. "This is only shiny paper," he whispered. "The trolls are just giving Grullo pieces of paper!"

Lucy turned to Danny, her eyes shining brightly. "Danny, my parents run a sweet stall."

"I know, Lucy."

"A *sweet* stall, Danny!"

"And so?"

"The sweets are wrapped in shiny paper… silver, gold, blue, red, green, all sorts of colours. You could promise Grullo lots of shiny paper in exchange for leaving Joey, the unicorns and all the children alone."

"Brilliant!" Danny cried. "Now I've just got to convince Grullo not to eat us."

In the end, it turned out to be very easy to persuade the giant. When Danny promised him as much shiny paper as he wanted, in any colour he liked, Grullo readily agreed to their conditions. He even carried them all the way back through the forest, to the very edge.

"I just hope Mum and Dad understand," Lucy sighed as they bounced along on the giant's hand, feeling a little seasick.

"I'm sure they will," Danny said reassuringly. At last they reached the spot where they had first met Argenta, and the giant gently placed them on the ground.

"Thanks Grullo," Danny said. "You wait over there under the trees and we'll go and get all the shiny paper for you." He turned to the others. "Tom, you and Lucy go and explain everything to Lucy's parents and start bringing the sweet wrappers here. I'll stay with Grullo, in case he changes his mind. We'll meet here later."

Lucy and Tom ran off. Lucinda flew over to a huge toadstool and sat down, holding her head in her hands. Joey rested his head against Danny's legs. "Sorry, Danny," he murmured. "If I hadn't been so stupid and bumped into Grullo, we could have got away without him catching us. I'm really sorry."

"It's OK," Danny reassured him, stroking his neck. "This way we got you back and we've made sure it won't happen again. Now we've just got to find your mum."

As he said this, Argenta stepped out from behind some trees. "I am here, Danny," she said quietly.

Joey gave a delighted whinny and galloped over to his mother. He rubbed his short horn against her face, hardly able to believe they were together again. The two remained close for some time, nuzzling each other and talking softly. Danny felt tears pricking his eyes.

"Joey has told me everything," Argenta said, walking over to him. "I thank you, Danny, my husband and I are forever in your debt. If I can ever be of assistance to you, just let me know."

Danny blushed. "Tom, Lucy, and Lucinda helped too," he muttered.

"And I thank them also," Argenta replied. Lucinda flew over to her and kissed her on the forehead.

"It was a wonderful adventure," she said, "if a little scary at times. I wouldn't have missed it for the world!"

"And the giant?" Argenta asked.

Danny pointed towards a particularly dense thicket of trees. "He's hiding in there."

Argenta walked over to the trees. "Giant!" she called in a stern voice. The leaves on the trees began shaking violently. "Giant, come out," she ordered.

There was a cracking noise as several branches broke, then the giant emerged from the trees. Out of the forest, he seemed bigger than ever. He stood at least seven metres tall and each leg was as wide as the thickest tree trunk. He could have swiped Argenta away with one sweep of his mighty hands, like someone swatting a fly, yet he stood shivering with fear before the unicorn.

"Giant, I hold no grudge against you," Argenta said kindly. "Unicorns and giants have always been at peace with one another. However," she continued, a fierce look coming over her face, "be warned... if you should ever cross my path again, I shall not be so lenient."

The giant nodded his head furiously, tears rolling down his huge cheeks.

"And tell the trolls to keep well away from the unicorns," Argenta added. "We will not tolerate this kind of behaviour."

The giant nodded again. "Grullo understand," he rumbled. "Grullo leave unicorns and children alone."

41

Danny began to feel sorry for the poor giant. "Come on, Grullo. Let's go and see if your shiny treasure is ready." He watched as the unicorns and Lucinda returned to the forest, thankful that the adventure was over. Joey looked back just before they entered the dark shadows. "See ya next time, Danny!" he shouted and then they were gone. Danny waved back, and led the giant away from the forest. With a sigh of relief he saw Tom, Lucy and many others from the fairground arriving, their arms loaded with sweet wrappers. Visibly shaking as they approached, Tom and Lucy's helpers placed the wrappers on the ground before the giant, then turned on their heels and practically ran back to the safety of the fairground.

Later, Danny watched Grullo disappear happily into the forest with an enormous sack full of shiny sweet papers grasped tightly in his left hand. Tucked under his right arm was the toy woolly mammoth Danny had won earlier, which Tom had brought over from his stall. Danny smiled, satisfied.

"So how did you like your first trip to Dreamland, Danny?" Tom asked."It was great! I can't wait until tomorrow night."

"We'll be here waiting for you," Lucy promised. "Let's hope it's a bit quieter next time!"

Chapter Three
The Magic Show

Danny sat in the front row of the audience, eagerly awaiting the start of the show. "There's lots of people here, Stupendo must be really good," he said to Tom, who was sitting next to him.

"Oh he is, just wait and see," the gnome replied. "Like I said, he's the greatest magician in Dreamland."

Lucy sat down beside Danny and handed them both their popcorn and drinks. "Sorry it took so much, there was a really long queue."

"That's OK, thanks, Lucy," Danny grinned. "I think you're just in time, look!"

The lights dimmed and music started playing. Everyone clapped as the curtains began to open, a few latecomers treading on people's toes as they hurried to their seats. Everything went quiet as a drum roll echoed around the theatre. A spotlight lit up the empty stage, turning it into a bright island surrounded by total darkness, then suddenly a tremendous bang shook the theatre and the stage filled with thick, white smoke. A figure stepped forward out of the haze wearing a long, purple cape and a tall hat, his arms stretched out wide.

The audience cheered wildly, while the magician removed his hat with a flourish and bowed solemnly. Danny watched, enraptured, as the show began. He had seen magic shows before, but none like this.

After pulling a large, white rabbit from his hat, Stupendo waved his wand and the animal remained suspended in mid-air. With a flick of his wand, the rabbit started dancing in time with some music, its ears flopping comically from side to side. When the music stopped, the rabbit rolled over a couple of times and then vanished into thin air. Stupendo put his hat back on his head and bowed. The audience's cheering turned to laughter as the rabbit reappeared from under the hat, its nose twitching as it too bowed. Then it jumped down to the floor and ran off the stage before Stupendo could catch it and put it back into his hat.

The whole show was full of surprises; every time Danny thought that Stupendo was doing a normal, everyday trick, the magician would wave his wand and something spectacular would happen. A bunch of flowers that came out of the end of his wand began sprouting green shoots until the whole stage was covered from top to bottom with plants. Just as some tendrils began entwining themselves around his legs, Stupendo clicked his fingers. There was a flash of light and the stage returned to normal, with no sign of any plants at all. Then a dove flew down from the ceiling and landed on his hand. The magician covered it carefully with a silk cloth and said a few words, moving his wand in a circular motion. The cloth changed shape and began to move, gently at first and then more vigorously. Stupendo whipped away the cloth and thousands of butterflies flew around the theatre over the audience's heads, before returning to the stage. They landed on Stupendo and covered him entirely, until he looked like a huge, shimmering tree. The lights turned off for a few seconds; when they came back on the butterflies were gone and Stupendo was stroking the dove once more.

Danny's hands ached from clapping so much and his throat was sore from cheering, but he was enjoying every minute of the show. As Stupendo took his final bow, the lights went up and the curtains slowly closed in front of him. Danny turned to Tom and Lucy, beaming broadly.

"He's fantastic!" he cried. "I've never seen anything like it!"

"He excelled himself tonight," Tom said. "Must be because you're here, Danny, he wanted to impress you."

"It was a terrific show," Danny replied. "I'm sorry it's over now."

Just then a girl ran over to them. "Stupendo asks if you and your friends would like to join him backstage?" she said to Danny.

"Yes, please!" they chorused and followed the girl backstage to Stupendo's dressing room. She opened the door and stood back to let them go by.

"Have fun!" she grinned.

"Thanks," Danny replied, as he, Tom and Lucy entered the room. Danny noticed a small, black rock on the floor just inside the door and stooped down to pick it up. As soon as he touched it, a blue light suddenly enveloped them and they felt themselves being lifted up, swirling round and round as if in the vortex of an enormous hurricane. It seemed to go on forever, the wind whistling in their ears as they spiralled ever higher. All of a sudden, they landed with a bump on a hard surface and the wind died down to a strong breeze.

"Wh-what was that?" Danny gasped, swaying slightly as his head continued spinning.

"I-I don't know," Tom answered, trying to stay upright. "Where are we?"

The night sky was pitch black above them and there was not a star to be seen. A dim light seemed to come from somewhere, though, as they could see each other's pale faces. Nothing stirred around them and the ground beneath their feet was dry and dusty. Lucy turned slowly around, trying to understand where they were.

"Oh!" she exclaimed. "Look here, you two."

Tom and Danny turned to face her, their mouths dropping open in amazement. There, far away in the night sky, they could see a beautiful blue and white globe.

"That's planet Earth," Lucy whispered. "We're on the Moon!"

Danny whistled softly. "So that's not the sky, that's outer space," he said, pointing upwards. "What I don't understand is how we can be here without space suits."

"Anything's possible in Dreamland," Tom said, smiling.

"I didn't create this," Danny said.

"So who did?"

"I've no idea. What are we supposed to do now?" he wondered.

Lucy tapped him on the shoulder. "There's a light over there," she said, gesturing towards a hill some distance away.

"Let's go there, then," Danny said.

After a long walk over rocky terrain, they arrived at the edge of a huge crater. Just beyond its further rim they could see the hill Lucy had pointed out earlier; the light seemed to come from behind it. They slowly made their way around the crater until they came to the bottom of a steep incline. Danny took a few steps forward but his feet couldn't get a grip in the loose scree that covered the slope and he slithered back down to the bottom again. He closed his eyes and imagined himself at the top of the hill, but when he opened them he was still standing at the bottom of the slope.

"We're not going to get up there," he gasped, red-faced. "Can you see any other way around?"

They searched carefully, but could find no other way to get past the hill to the source of the light.

Tom sighed. "I don't think we're going to get there. We might as well give up and go home."

"How do we get back?" Danny asked. The other two stared at him, the awful truth suddenly dawning on them. Danny had no power over their actions in this world and had no way of getting them home. Tom kicked angrily at the slope, almost falling over backwards.

"Watch out, Tom!" Lucy yelled, as the hillside collapsed and began to slide down towards them. The gnome jumped out of the way just in time, as a huge pile of stones and earth landed where he had been standing a moment before.

"Oh, well done, Tom," Danny laughed.

"Wh-what do you mean?" Tom asked, puzzled.

"Look." Danny pointed at the hillside. Tom turned and saw that the dislodged scree had uncovered a flight of stone steps cut into the hill, all the way to the top.

"You've found us a way up," Lucy giggled.

"Well, let's go then," Tom said, heading up the steps.

When they got to the top, they could see for miles all around. Behind them lay the crater amid the rocks and boulders on the Moon's dusty surface. Before them lay a beautiful valley bathed in bright sunshine, full of weird and wonderful plants and animals. Even stranger, though, were the colours. The grass was purple, the trees all different shades of orange and lilac, and the sky was yellow. An odd, giraffe-like creature with dark blue fur ambled across a pink stream, its long, spindly legs trembling against the force of the water. It dipped its head and drank deeply, beads of pink liquid dripping from its mouth.

Danny looked at Lucy and Tom. "This is getting weirder and weirder. No one lives on the Moon!"

"Let's go down and take a closer look," Tom said excitedly. They strode down the grassy slope, marvelling at all the bizarre things they could see. As their legs brushed through the long grass, small, hopping insects leapt up out of the undergrowth, jumping as high as their heads, then curled themselves up into tiny balls and rolled away out of sight among the blades of grass. Danny started laughing, then stopped to stare as an enormous, crimson toad lumbered on top of a stone and began lazily flicking its tongue, catching the small insects as they fled past. It gazed solemnly back at Danny, blinking first one amber eye and then the other, slowly swallowing its meal.

Danny carried on down the slope, keeping an eye out for other strange creatures that could be hiding in the undergrowth. At the bottom there was a white path that wound along the valley, beside the stream. A herd of the giraffe-like animals was grazing nearby and seemed totally unaware that Danny, Tom, and Lucy were walking towards them. Several animals were stood beneath a tall tree, using their long tongues to strip the orange leaves off its branches.

As the three friends walked through the valley, they could see monstrous fish swimming in the stream, with sharp teeth that glinted malevolently in the sparkling water. As they all watched, a huge fish lifted itself out of the stream, its rainbow-coloured scales glistening with drops of water, and launched itself at the riverbank. It returned to the stream with a crimson toad dangling from its mouth and disappeared from view.

"That was impressive!" Tom gasped, stepping away from the edge of the bank.

"Very." Danny looked a bit pale.

"Let's keep going," Lucy suggested, "before one of those fish thinks about trying to eat us!"

The path led them to a wooden hut that had been built against a hillock. A large, leafy tree full of turquoise fruit provided shade from the bright sunlight.

The three friends stopped outside the hut. "Try knocking on the door, Danny," Lucy whispered.

"OK," Danny replied, also speaking softly.

"Why are you both whispering?" Tom asked loudly. The other two looked at him in surprise.

"I don't know," Danny said. "It's just this place… it's like being in a church or something. It makes you want to talk quietly."

Lucy raised her eyebrows. "Can't you feel it, Tom?"

The gnome shrugged. "All I know is that I'd like some answers as to why we're here and what this place is."

"You only have to ask," came a grumpy voice from behind them. They wheeled around, startled. The door of the hut was open and a small, wizened man was standing in the doorway. He held a heavy, black cape clasped tightly around him so that only his head was visible. Fine, grey wisps of hair covered his scalp and his leathery face was a mass of deep wrinkles, making him appear impossibly old. His startling blue eyes, however, were full of vitality as they darted from

Danny to Tom and then Lucy. Nobody moved or spoke and the air between them became filled with tension.

Chapter Four
The Man In The Moon

"Who-who are you?" Danny asked, his voice trembling slightly.

The old man gazed at him. "My name is Stythwhirr Jhmkyrwit," he replied, "but I also answer to Jim."

"Pleased to meet you, Sty... Styth... er, Jim," Danny stammered. "I'm Danny, this is Lucy, and this is Tom."

"I know," Jim said. "Come on in, then, don't want to be standing out here all day." He shuffled back inside the hut without even glancing at them. The three friends followed him in, blinking rapidly as their eyes tried to adjust to the dim interior.

"Sit down, you're making the place look untidy," Jim said, pointing at some chairs. He sat in a rocking chair near a roaring fire. "When you get to my age, you feel the cold more." He pulled a blanket around his shoulders. "Now then, you're probably wondering what I am doing here on the Moon. I will explain things to you, but I will not tolerate interruptions."

Danny cleared his throat. "We were, um, very surprised to find this valley. We've always been told the Moon is uninhabitable, with no atmosphere or water."

Jim smirked. "In fact, this little oasis is the only habitable place on the Moon," he said. "We created it many millennia ago."

"We?" Tom asked. "Who are you?"

"I told you, I am Jim."

"No, *who* are you, where do you come from?"

"Now you're asking too many questions," the old man complained. He sighed heavily. "My race came to this solar system many millions of years ago, when the Earth was newly formed. We planted the first seeds of life on your planet and have been here watching its evolution ever since."

"You've been watching us?" Danny exclaimed.

"Yes. I suppose you could say that this is an observation station. Many generations of my family have lived here in this artificial dome, keeping an eye on things. I took over from my father two hundred thousand years ago, and my son will arrive within the next century to take over from me."

"*Two hundred thousand years*!" Danny cried.

"Yes, dear boy. And please stop repeating everything I say, it's almost as annoying as being interrupted. My race lives a lot longer than you humans."

"I'm sorry," Danny said, blushing. "I just meant... that's an awful long time to be up here by yourself."

"I'm not by myself, I have my herd of Planktars to keep me company," Jim replied. He saw their puzzled faces. "Those creatures in the valley, you must have seen them on your way here."

"Yes, we did, but they can't talk to you… can they?" Danny asked, not sure of anything any more.

"No, they don't speak, but most of the time I find that a blessing. We are a solitary race and tire quickly of talkative company." He glared at them to underline his point.

"What is your race called?" Tom said, unable to resist asking another question.

"We call ourselves Arkans and we come from a planet many, many light years away, called Kwercian."

"You're the man in the Moon!" Danny said excitedly. "Just like in the nursery rhyme!"

Jim shook his head. "Can't say that I've heard of it," he grunted, scowling fiercely at Danny. The boy blushed bright red.

"How have you managed to remain hidden from us?" Lucy asked, trying to change the subject to save Danny's embarrassment.

"So many questions," Jim said irritably. "Up until recently, it was very easy. We made our base here on the hidden side of the Moon, the side that people from Earth can never see. But then you entered the space age in the sixties and started sending up satellites that circle the Moon. I had to develop a rudimentary screening device that worked very well at the time, but there are many more satellites now, which makes it more difficult for me to carry on staying here undetected. I think our time here on the Moon is almost up and we will have to leave you to grow up by yourselves."

"Do you know how we got here today?" Lucy asked. "Danny usually creates the places we visit, but he says he had nothing to do with us coming here."

"What do you mean, he *creates* places?" Jim asked, curious.

"He has a ticket that takes him to Dreamland when he goes to sleep. We all meet up and have great adventures," Lucy explained.

"I have no idea what Dreamland is, and I have no idea how you got here," Jim replied. "I thought you had arrived on one of your spaceships. I was rather hoping you wouldn't find your way up the hill and turn around and go home. As I said, we Arkans don't like company and it is rather tiring having to explain everything to you."

"I know how we got here," Danny said suddenly. "I picked up a rock on the floor, I thought maybe Stupendo had dropped it and I wanted to give it back to him. Then that blue light appeared and we found ourselves here. Obviously this is all still part of Dreamland," he added to the others.

"A rock, you say," Jim muttered. "It must have been a Moon rock. The Moon seems dead and lifeless, but there is more to this boulder than you'd think. If it has the ability to transport people here just by touching a part of it, that would be a remarkable discovery, very remarkable indeed." His voice died away as he closed his eyes in concentration.

Just as Danny, Tom, and Lucy thought he had gone to sleep, he suddenly sat up. "We must do some experiments," he said enthusiastically, and then he glared at Danny. "There is nothing obvious in this world, son. Like I said, I have never heard of Dreamland before."

The little man moved amazingly quickly for someone so old, and Danny, Tom, and Lucy found that they had to run to keep up with him. He followed the path back along the valley, retracing the route they had taken earlier. They passed more of the strange, giraffe-like creatures and Danny couldn't help asking Jim about them.

"They keep me company here," he answered. "I can use their fur to make blankets and clothes and I can drink their milk and make other foods with it. I suppose I am like the shepherds with their flocks of sheep on Earth."

"Strange sheep," Tom muttered to Danny.

"What about the fish?" Lucy asked. "Do you eat them?"

"No, they don't taste very nice," Jim replied, shuddering. "But they are an essential part of the eco-system here… without them the dome's delicate balance would be upset and the whole place would become uninhabitable for my people."

"Why…?" Lucy began, but Jim snorted angrily and walked even more quickly, leaving them behind. When they arrived at the foot of the hill again, Jim veered to the left and went along the bottom of the slope until he came to a cave. He disappeared inside a small opening without waiting to see if the others were following him. They ducked down to get through the gap and crawled along a narrow tunnel until they arrived in a large cavern. It was brightly lit and full of computers. Jim rushed from machine to machine, pressing buttons and checking monitors.

"This is where I keep an eye on you humans," he said, still busy with the computers. "I have cameras attached to all the satellites, it's very easy nowadays for me to see what's going on. Look here." He pointed at one of the monitors.

Danny's eyes opened wide in astonishment as he peered closely at the screen. "That's my house!" he exclaimed. "Look, Tom, Lucy, there's the tree house I told you about, and there's my old swing under the apple tree…" He put his hand over his mouth as Jim zoomed the camera in even closer. "That's my mum," he said, watching as she turned the TV off and made her way upstairs to bed. Tom and Lucy were equally impressed.

"That's enough for now," Jim muttered, turning the monitor off. He reached over and pressed a large, red button, clapping his hands in satisfaction. "There!" He turned to Danny, Tom, and Lucy. "I've sent a robot out to get a sample of Moon rock. Then it will bring it back here and we can run some tests on it. Now, we wait."

They sat in uncomfortable silence until a whirring noise signalled the return of the robot. It hovered in the air before Jim, its metal pincers holding a glass container with a lump of black rock inside it. Jim took the jar and placed it inside a complicated-looking piece of machinery. The robot glided off to the back of the cavern and turned itself off.

"This machine will run various tests on the piece of rock," Jim said, his eyes gleaming. "It won't take long."

Danny, Tom, and Lucy watched as lights flashed on the front of the machine and it made beeping sounds. Then it went silent and some strange symbols appeared on a nearby monitor.

"Ha!" Jim shouted, startling them. "Just as I thought! The rock's properties make it a very powerful magnet, which is attracted to the Moon's core. It uses heat as a catalyst to create enough energy to activate it and once activated, it turns into a transportation device. Your hand was hot enough to power the device, which is why that bit of rock brought you here when you touched it. This is an amazing discovery which will be of great importance to my people." He turned to Danny, surprising him with a huge smile on his craggy face. "We can easily reverse the polarity so that we can use it to send us home. It will save us many light years of travel between Kwercian and the Moon. Perhaps we can even adapt it so it can be used to explore other solar systems. The possibilities are endless."

"Can you use it to send us back to Dreamland?" Tom asked.

"Of course," Jim said scornfully. "Reversing the polarity of your rock will take you back to where you came from." He pressed some buttons on the machine, which beeped several times. "There, it's ready."

Danny looked at Tom and Lucy. "Shall we go, then? Stupendo will be wondering where we are."

"Thank you so much for everything," Lucy said to Jim. "We've had a lovely visit."

"Yes, yes," the old man replied, squirming uncomfortably. "It's been, er, nice, I suppose." He glared at the three of them. "Make sure you don't tell anyone about me, I don't want them sending any more probes up here," he growled.

"Oh, don't worry, I don't think anyone's going to believe us if we say there really is a man in the Moon," Danny laughed.

Jim glared at him. "Why do you keep calling me the man in the Moon?"

"Well, you know, it's like the nursery rhyme," Danny replied. "You must have heard it."

"Enlighten me," Jim ordered.

Danny began reciting:

"The man in the Moon,
Came down too soon
And asked the way to Norwich.
He went by the south
And burned his mouth
By eating cold plum porridge."

"You *must* know it," he added.

"It can't be about me," Jim said. "I've never been to Norwich and I can't stand porridge. So please stop mentioning it."

"Sorry," Danny said nervously. "It was just a joke."

"Not a very good one," Jim muttered, with a glint in his eye. He turned away, busying himself with his computers, but Danny could have sworn that he saw the old man smiling.

"Now," Jim said, "all you have to do is touch the rock and it will take all three of you back to where you came from." He headed back into the tunnel without looking at them. "I hate goodbyes," he said gruffly and disappeared from view.

"This has been the weirdest adventure yet," Tom said.

"You can say that again!" Danny agreed. He held his hand above the rock and looked at his friends. "Ready?" he asked. Tom and Lucy gave him the thumbs up. He lowered his hand.

There was another flash of blue light and they found themselves once more in Stupendo's dressing room. The magician was staring at them, open-mouthed.

"Where did you come from?" he asked in amazement. "I was about to give up waiting for you."

"You wouldn't believe us," Danny said, laughing.

After they had explained everything to Stupendo, they asked his opinion on how they may have ended up on the Moon.

"Are you sure you didn't create the adventure, Danny?" he asked. Danny shook his head. Stupendo thought for a while. "Do you ever have dreams that seem so real that the morning after you're unsure whether you dreamt it or if it really happened? Perhaps there is another part of Dreamland yet unexplored, where people like Jim exist. Or perhaps it was just part of this Dreamland and you are unaware that you created it. I really don't know."

When Danny looked out of his window early the next morning, he could see the Moon still high in the sky.

Do you really exist, Jim, or was it just part of my dream? he wondered. *Maybe I'll get the chance to go up in a rocket one day and find out for myself.* He paused as a thought struck him. "How on earth did that piece of Moon rock end up in Stupendo's dressing room, just as we were there?" he said out loud.

He got dressed and went downstairs for breakfast, happy that it was Saturday and Mike was coming over later. Maybe they could pretend the tree house was a spaceship and go in search of the planet Kwercian...

Chapter Five
The Cavemen

Danny yawned as he brushed his teeth sleepily. Several weeks had passed since his first visit to Dreamland and he had had lots of wonderful adventures there. He smiled as he remembered being the captain of a fine pirate ship and how he had made Tom walk the plank. Tom's face had been a picture when he reappeared over the ship's rail, dripping wet and spluttering indignantly.

Then there was the time he and Lucy had turned into eagles (Tom hadn't wanted to go) and flown all around Dreamland. He had loved the wild feeling of freedom and happiness as they soared high above barren mountaintops, tropical rainforests, wide open seas and glittering blue lakes. He and Lucy had talked about it for hours afterwards, until Tom had crossly told them to shut up. Yes, he'd had some great times!

"What will you dream about tonight, Danny?" his mum asked as she gave him his goodnight kiss.

"Dunno," mumbled Danny, already falling asleep. His mum smiled and closed the bedroom door.

Images of a winding river flowing through a moonlit landscape flew around Danny as he fell down through the mist. When he finally came to a stop, he found

63

himself standing a few metres away from the entrance to a cave. The sun was setting behind some trees, the sky glowing red and orange in the fading daylight. To his right, he could hear waves crashing onto a nearby beach, and as he moved his feet he could hear pebbles crunching beneath them. A cold wind began to blow as the sky grew darker, making him shiver.

Suddenly, he heard a commotion to his left. Turning, he saw several men running towards him out of a wood, carrying axes and spears. He hardly had time to register what was happening before they were upon him, dragging him roughly into the cave, his heart beating wildly with fear. The men pushed him roughly to one side, letting him fall in an untidy heap on the floor whilst they started rolling a huge stone across the cave entrance. Danny heard a blood-curdling roar from outside and something threw itself at the stone with a loud THUD! He glimpsed a clawed foot trying to reach into the cave, then there was a sudden yelp as the stone rolled into place. His heart beat painfully in his chest as he noticed several shadowy figures standing near him, lit up by the flickering, orange glow of several fires. There was a moment's silence, in which the only sound was the noise of the men's laboured breathing, and then a confusion of excited voices broke out from behind him. Danny realised there were many more people further back in the cave and tried to press himself against the rocky wall, hoping they wouldn't see him, but it was too late.

"Come," a man grunted, pulling him towards the others. The cave opened out into an enormous open space, the ceiling so high above them that Danny couldn't even see it. Several fires were blazing, each one with a group of people sat around it. Danny jumped back with shock as he saw his captors' faces clearly for the first time. Their prominent brows and facial features were strangely ape-like, as were their short, muscular bodies. There were about thirty people altogether, men, women and children. All had long, uncombed hair and wore animal skins.

'Neanderthals!' he thought excitedly, looking around the cave. He had just finished reading a book about prehistoric men and now he had created them in his Dreamland! He saw a group of older women sitting close to one fire, staring and pointing at him and grinning wide, toothless grins. As he watched, a young child approached them carrying what looked like mashed fruit in a bowl. Startled, he realised that the bowl was in fact the top half of an animal's skull, scoured and cleaned so that it could be used to hold food. The women greedily scooped the fruit into their mouths with their fingers, eating with great relish.

Several men and women drew near Danny, talking softly amongst themselves. A woman reached out and touched his short, blond hair, then ran a slightly grubby finger along his cheek.

"You different. You like others over there." She pointed to two forms on the floor, lying wrapped in animal skins. Danny peered at them.

"Tom! Lucy! You're here too!" he exclaimed. The cavemen jumped back as he ran over to his friends and shook them awake.

"Danny!" they cried when they saw him. "You made it then."

Tom explained that they had arrived a little while before and had decided to lie down quietly and wait for him. "We must have fallen asleep," he said, "it was so warm and cosy under those furs."

"At least you're here now," Lucy said happily. "They seem really friendly, don't they?"

"Friendly?" Danny said, remembering how they had run at him, brandishing weapons. "I wouldn't say that, exactly."

A young man came towards them. "We no want to hurt you," he grunted. "Big animal outside, *he* hurt you. We save you, bring you in cave."

"Oh," Danny said, embarrassed. "Sorry. It was a bit of a shock, you know."

The man nodded. "You all come, eat now," he said, pointing to a nearby fire.

"Thanks," Danny replied gratefully. He turned to Lucy. "How come we can all understand each other?" he whispered. "Cavemen didn't talk like us."

"Well, it's your Dreamland," she answered. "You must have created them like this. It does make life a lot easier, though, doesn't it?"

"It's a good job I made them friendly too!" he muttered, as they went to sit by the fire with the caveman's family. The bright glow hurt Danny's eyes after the gloominess of the cave and it took him a few minutes to adjust. Blinking, he looked at the family sitting before him; their features were softened by the shadows, but he could make out the prominent brows and flat noses familiar to him from his text books.

The young caveman turned to him. "I Totom, this wife Orta and these children Ramda and Urdi," he said hesitantly.

"Pleased to meet you," Danny replied. He, Tom and Lucy smiled at a young woman with long, black hair, dressed in heavy animal skins to protect her from the cold, and two small children, similarly dressed, holding onto her skirt. Ramda, the girl, looked exactly like her mother and smiled shyly back at them. Urdi, her younger brother, sucked furiously on his thumb and hid his face behind his mother's legs. Orta pointed at the fire.

"I cook food for you, we eat now," she said and picked up several bundles, handing one to each of them. Danny found he was holding a very hot parcel of leaves. He opened it and a wonderful aroma of herbs, berries and roasted fish hit him. His mouth watering, he hungrily ate the fish, surprised at how good it tasted. After a while they all sat back, licking their oily fingers and wishing that they had more.

"It good, yes?" Totom asked, pleased that they had so obviously liked it. "Orta best cook here." The young woman blushed and playfully hit her husband.

"He exaggerate," she said, embarrassed. "Totom, you take them to meet others now."

After they had thanked Orta profusely, Totom led them to the neighbouring fires, introducing them to everyone. They all offered the three friends something to eat and Danny thought he had never tasted such good food. Wild berries cooked with honey in small, hollowed-out stones, tiny roasted birds with stewed root vegetables, fish cooked in a variety of ways and many more wonderful things.

"I'll never eat again!" Lucy groaned, rubbing her stomach.

"I will," Tom grinned, tucking into a bowl of vegetable broth with great gusto while a caveman watched him, nudging his wife with pride.

"Who are those people?" Danny whispered to Totom, nodding towards a group of elderly men sitting together at the back of the cave.

"They are elders, wise men," Totom replied. "They talk, decide what tribe do, where tribe go. They speak with you, they need help."

"OK." Danny wondered what he could help them with. He didn't have to wait long to find out.

"Welcome to our cave, Danny," the oldest man said softly. "We are very glad that you have come, we have a problem you can help us with."

"What can I do?" Danny asked.

"We have been living in this cave for many seasons now," the wise man began. "My son Totom was born here, as were his children. I myself arrived from a land a great distance from here, a harsh land where living was very difficult. Here we have lots of food to eat… fish we can catch in the sea, berries and vegetables we can gather on the land and an abundance of animals we can hunt, and our tribe has prospered. But now the sea is getting closer to our cave with every new season and soon it will arrive at the entrance. We must find somewhere else to live before that happens. A new home where we can be as happy as we are here."

"You must be very sorry to have to leave here," Danny said sadly. "It won't be easy to find another cave like this one."

"This is true. But unfortunately, we have no choice. We must leave as soon as possible."

"How can I help?" Danny asked.

"We need as many of our men here as possible to guard the cave against the wild animals. They are attacking us more and more, they know we have many young that are defenceless. Perhaps you and your two friends could search for a new cave for us, further inland? We will send two men with you to protect you against attacks, of course," he added.

"I'll have to speak with Tom and Lucy first and ask them if they are willing to come with me," Danny replied.

"Of course you must," the wise man replied.

Danny made his way back to where Tom and Lucy were looking at some children's shell collections. One child had made small holes in several shells and strung them onto a cord to make a necklace. She was tying it around Lucy's neck as Danny approached.

"Oh, thank you, it's beautiful," Lucy smiled. "Look Danny, what a lovely gift."

Danny nodded. It really was magnificent; each spiral-shaped shell had been polished until it glimmered in the firelight and a lot of care had been taken to arrange them in a pretty pattern. Lucy gently touched the necklace. Then she removed a glittery hair-slide from her hair, and handed it to the girl.

"I didn't make it myself, but I hope you like it anyway," she said. The girl squealed in delight and ran off to show it to her mother, who was standing nearby.

"I think she liked it," Lucy beamed.

Danny beckoned Tom over, who was now tasting a delicious apple stew, and quickly explained the situation to them both.

"So, what do we do?" he asked. "It could be a dangerous journey."

"If we can go into the Dark Forest and come out again safely, we can do this!" Lucy exclaimed.

"You know, you can change all of this if you wanted to," Tom said hesitantly. "You couldn't in the Dark Forest as that wasn't part of your dream, but all this comes from your imagination. Just close your eyes and you can make the sea recede far enough so that they can stay here."

"I'd already thought of that, but I'd prefer to carry on with this adventure and see how things develop. It'll be more of a challenge." Danny laughed. "And maybe we can find them an even better place, safe from all the wild animals."

Tom sighed. "I thought you were going to take the easy option for a moment. I should know by now how much you like a challenge. And putting us in danger," he added.

"We can always change it later on, if things go wrong," Lucy reminded them, ever the practical one.

"After all their hospitality, I suppose the least we can do is try." Tom patted his stomach and grinned at Danny. "Maybe it won't be that dangerous... and we will have two of them to protect us, so we should be all right."

"So, we're agreed then?" Danny asked. Lucy and Tom nodded enthusiastically, excited at the prospect of another adventure. The three of them made their way over to the wise men to tell them the good news and within minutes, everyone in the cave knew that Danny, Tom, and Lucy had agreed to help them.

Suddenly, a slow, haunting melody echoed around the cave. Danny spotted the musician standing near a fire in the middle of the cave. Moving nearer, he could see that the caveman was blowing into a rudimentary whistle made from an animal's shin-bone. By using his fingers to cover a combination of three holes which had been bored in the hollow bone, and by widening or narrowing the space between his lips, he could produce a surprising variety of notes.

Two more cavemen joined the musician; one held two smooth sticks in his hands, the other two fist-sized rocks, which they began banging together rhythmically. As the tempo got faster and faster and the music became more joyful, several cavewomen started dancing around the trio, swaying backwards and forwards in time with the music. The melody surged through the three friends, filling them with hope and courage for their upcoming adventure.

Danny, Tom, and Lucy weren't feeling quite so brave a little while later. They were standing before the large stone still covering the entrance to the cave, with warm animal skins over the top of their own clothes and armed with short, dagger-like weapons. Totom and his brother Midam stood at their sides, proudly holding long spears and obviously enjoying all the attention.

Some of the cavemen walked forward and began rolling back the stone. Outside they could see thousands of stars glittering brightly in the sky, even though it was almost dawn. The Moon hung high above them, an enormous silver orb quietly watching over the sleeping world below.

"We wish you luck," the wise men said. "May Okram protect you and guide you."

"Okram?" Tom whispered.

"It must be their God," Lucy replied. "Ssshh."

The oldest wise man stepped forward and daubed their foreheads with red ochre. "Oh Okram, guide our friends in the right direction and protect them from danger. Bring them back to us swiftly and with good news," he intoned. The other wise men bowed their heads.

"Hear us, Okram," they chanted. "Help us, Okram. Save us, Okram." The other cavemen began to chant too, over and over again, until the whole cave echoed with their voices.

"That's some send-off," Danny remarked to Lucy.

She smiled back at him. "Let's hope we're worth it," she replied quietly as they headed out of the cave, Totom and Midam leading the way.

The sun had already risen over the horizon and the Moon and the stars had disappeared. Now that it was daylight, they could see the cavemen's home properly. The cave was set in a cliff that sloped down to the water's edge, where small waves gently washed onto a pebble beach that sloped up to its front. Maritime pines dotted the coastline, their fragrant scent mingling with the more pungent smell of the sea. They could see that the ocean was indeed eroding the coastline – dried seaweed and other debris had been left by the tide just a few metres from the cave mouth.

The five explorers set out on their journey. Totom and Midam led them to the wood where Danny had seen the cavemen run out from the day before, looking anxiously about for ferocious animals. As they walked through the wood, brightly coloured birds flitted unceasingly among the high trees, filling the air with the sound of their twittering. Flowers of all kinds covered the ground, their scented perfume attracting a multitude of insects - enormous butterflies competed fiercely with loudly humming bees for the flowers' sweet nectar.

Huge ferns covered the ground beneath the trees and they could hear rustling noises as small creatures scrambled about in the undergrowth.Danny looked back towards the cave, already small in the distance and could just make out the sea shimmering beyond it. As he watched, several children ran out of the cave and launched themselves into the water, their screams of laughter barely audible.

"We need to find somewhere near a river or a lake, with plenty of fish and lots of space for the children to run around," he said.

"There is a river," Totom replied. "We already follow it a little, but no find new home." He pointed to his right and Danny saw a silver ribbon of water threading its way through the trees. Dense, tightly packed vegetation grew right down to the water's edge, leaving no space where the cavemen could make a home.

"How far did you go?" he asked.

"We reach high cliff where water falls down, Okram no want us go further, he make water boil so we no pass. We no upset Okram," Midam replied.

"Perhaps we can climb up the cliff and see what's beyond," Lucy suggested.

"It's definitely worth having a look," Danny agreed. This adventure was starting to get exciting!

Chapter Six
New Lands

They set off again, trying to stay as close to the river as possible. It was quieter close to the water, as all sound was muffled by the thick foliage. Monkey-like animals jumped around in the trees, chattering excitedly at the newcomers and then scampering away again as they drew near.

Totom and Midam led the way, cutting a path through the thick vegetation with some crude but effective axes. After a long, tiring walk they heard a deep, rumbling sound in the distance.

"Grullo!" Lucy exclaimed.

"Nope, waterfall," Danny laughed. As they made their way around the next bend of the river, they saw that he was right. A churning expanse of frothy water poured down a high, sheer cliff, descending with a thundering roar into a large lake which emptied into the river.

"It's beautiful," Lucy whispered, overwhelmed by the scene before her. She understood why the cavemen had been afraid to go any further, the water really did look as if it was boiling. She turned to see Totom and Midam rooted to the ground in fear, staring wide-eyed at the waterfall.

"We scared, we make Okram angry," Totom said nervously. "See how he stirs water, he no want we go there." Midam nodded in agreement.

"Tom, Lucy, and I could climb up and see what's at the top while you two stay here and wait for us," Danny suggested. The two cavemen didn't want to let them go at first, but eventually agreed when they saw how determined Danny was. They held back as the three friends approached the waterfall, too scared to go any closer.

Danny looked up at the cliff before them, watching gallons of water pouring over the top. The air around them was damp with spray and the cliff's rocky surface was wet and slippery. The noise was deafening and the ground vibrated with the force of the falling water. He tugged Tom's arm.

"How are we going to get up there?" he yelled, trying to make himself heard over the din. "It looks impossible."

Tom pointed to a ledge halfway up, to the right of the waterfall. "There is a way up over there," he shouted back. "I'll lead, you and Lucy put your hands and feet exactly where I put mine." They walked over to where Tom had indicated, and found that the rock face was full of cracks and crevices.

"If we're careful, we should be able to climb up," Tom bellowed. "Follow me." He led the way slowly up the cliff face, somehow managing to find foot and hand holds in the rocky surface. Lucy followed him, her face pale but determined, and Danny went last. After a while he looked back down and his stomach lurched as he saw the water frothing and foaming far below him. He gulped and began climbing again, sweat beading his brow.

All of a sudden, Tom's strong arms reached down and pulled him up onto the ledge they had noticed earlier. The three of them sat down, their backs against the cliff edge, trying to catch their breath. Lucy reached out and caught some water in her cupped hands, eagerly drinking the fresh, clear liquid. Tom and Danny copied her, thirsty after their long climb. After a short rest, they once again made their way carefully up the cliff.

At long last they arrived at the top. They stood up and gazed around in wonder. A vast, fertile plain stretched for miles before them. The wide river snaked its way across the middle, with many smaller streams criss-crossing the plain to join it. Lush, green meadows gave way to dense woods, the cool shade beneath the trees offering welcome respite from the hot sun, and in the distance they could just make out the shadowy forms of gently sloping hills.

"We're sure to find a place here!" Lucy exclaimed. "It looks perfect."

"Remember, we need a cave that's easy to defend and with plenty of food for the cavemen to eat," Danny said. "And now I suppose we'll have to persuade our friends to come up," he added.

Tom glanced at him. "They won't want to climb the waterfall."

"Well they'll have to, they have to help us find a new home for them," Danny said crossly. He was beginning to feel tired and grumpy.

"I'll go down and persuade them to come up," Tom offered. He went back to the edge of the waterfall and looked down. "It could take me some time, though."

Lucy coughed. "Danny, why don't you create some ropes? We can attach them to that tree over there and Tom and the cavemen can use them to climb up."

Danny nodded. He closed his eyes and imagined three ropes, long enough to reach the bottom of the waterfall. When he opened his eyes, there were three thick ropes coiled at his feet. His chest swelled with pride and he grinned at Lucy and Tom. "Did you see what I can do?" he boasted.

"It's only some rope, Danny," Lucy said bluntly.

Danny's face fell. He picked up the ends of the ropes and took them over to the tree. Tom helped him tie them securely to the trunk, then they threw the ends over the side of the cliff. Danny and Lucy watched anxiously as Tom made his way back down the waterfall. Eventually he reached the bottom and they saw him talking animatedly to Totom and Midam.

After much gesturing and intense conversation, the two cavemen followed him over to the ropes. They reluctantly made their way up the cliff, occasionally slipping as they failed to find a foothold, until finally three heads appeared over the top, their faces dirty with sweat. Danny and Lucy helped them up, laughing at their astonished expressions as the two cavemen caught sight of the countryside that stretched before them.

"The waterfall wasn't a barrier, it was a test," Danny said. "Okram wanted to make sure you earned the right to a new home!" He pointed at the water. "If we follow the river's course, we should find somewhere for your tribe to live."

Totom and Midam looked around in wonder. "This Okram's kingdom," Midam whispered. "We safe here, find good home and good hunting ground. Our children grow big and strong. We happy here." He strode forward, Totom following closely behind. Danny, Tom, and Lucy exchanged smiles and followed them.

They travelled a long way; at times the river narrowed to a trickling stream, only to suddenly expand into an enormous lake around the next curve, forcing them to walk miles around its edge until they found the river again. They stopped to eat in a picturesque copse of elm trees, their mouths watering at the aroma of the food Orta had prepared for them. With full stomachs, they set off again, laughing and talking, their optimism renewed as they could see the hills rising in front of them. The two cavemen quickened the pace, with Danny, Lucy, and Tom trotting behind.

They didn't stop until they came to the foot of the first hill. Here the river flowed faster and their eyes grew wider as they saw enormous shoals of fish swimming in the current, their scales glistening in the water. Birds flew overhead and they could hear animals rustling in the undergrowth beneath the trees. Bushes laden with fruit and berries grew abundantly and Danny noticed wild corn growing in a meadow. He turned as he heard Lucy scream in delight.

"A cave!" she cried. "Look Danny, a cave in the hillside!"

They all ran excitedly to the entrance and went inside to explore. It was fresh and dry inside the cave and there was no sign of other inhabitants, animal or otherwise. Even better, they found a system of tunnels that burrowed deep into the hill which would offer them protection in case of attack.

"This our new home," Totom declared some time later. "Plenty big for everyone, plenty food and water. Thank you, Danny." He hugged the surprised boy.

"You're welcome," Danny laughed. "Now we just have to go back and get everyone."

Tom cleared his throat. "Ahem. What about using your Dreamland powers to get us back in the blink of an eye, Danny?"

"That's for wimps, Tom," Danny laughed. "Besides, the exercise will do you good!" he added, patting the gnome's ample stomach.

"Not funny," Tom grumbled, scowling as Lucy giggled.

It was getting dark again by the time they arrived back at the waterfall. They all climbed carefully down, using the ropes Danny had created earlier, and made their way back along the river towards the cave on the seashore.

"Danny, I think something's following us," Tom said after a while. They all stopped and listened.

"I can't hear anything," Danny whispered back.

"I definitely heard something," Tom insisted. They carried on walking, concentrating on the undergrowth around them.

A dark shape loomed in front of them. "We're back at the cave," Lucy said, relieved. She clapped her hands and broke into a run. At the same moment, a huge, growling animal came crashing out of the bushes, aiming straight at her. Lucy screamed in terror. The animal raised its leg and clawed at her arm, leaving a deep wound that poured with blood. As she fell back, half-fainting with fear and pain, Midam ran towards the beast with his spear held poised to strike. Jumping forward, Danny and Tom pulled Lucy away just as the animal attacked again.

There was a confusion of snarling growls and human voices as Midam and Totom fought the animal, stabbing it with their spears and daggers. Danny could see its long, sharp fangs and claws slashing through the air, aiming for the cavemen's throats while trying to dodge their weapons. The animal's snarls grew louder and more ferocious as it thrashed desperately about, its sides running with blood from the wounds inflicted by the cavemen. Danny watched as it gathered itself for one final attack, leaping at Midam's throat. The caveman stepped back and calmly held his spear before him, aimed at the animal's chest. There was an agonised scream and the beast was lying at Midam's feet, two spears sticking out of its body.

Midam wiped the sweat off his brow and grinned at Tom and Danny.

"He no bother us again," he said, smiling grimly. Then he looked at Lucy and became serious once more. "She need help," he said, picking her up in his arms. "I take her to cave."

Totom beckoned to Danny and Tom. "Women at cave help her, she get better. You two help me, we carry beast back to cave."

Danny looked down at the dead animal. "What is it?"

"Sabre-toothed tiger," Totom replied. "There many in woods."

"Now he tells us," Tom muttered.

Totom pointed to the beast. "Carry," he ordered.

Twenty minutes later, feeling very tired and dirty, Danny, Tom and Totom managed to drag the animal's carcass inside the cave. They were greeted by several women, who hurried them over to Orta. Her face was taut with worry.

"She no stop bleeding, herbs no work," she said, gesturing towards Lucy. Danny knelt down beside her, noticing the blood-stained leaves wrapped around her arm. She was unconscious and her breathing was shallow.

"She's in shock," Tom said. "Do something, Danny, please. This time you have to use your powers."

Danny closed his eyes and concentrated on making Lucy better. Then he opened them again and gazed hopefully at her, but her condition was unchanged. He tried again and again, but with no success. He looked around helplessly at the others.

"I don't know what to do," he murmured. The cavemen and women stared at him, trusting him to help Lucy. The firelight flickered, illuminating rudimentary drawings on the cave wall. Danny's heart leapt as he recognised one of the images. "Argill!" he breathed. He fixed his eyes on the picture, concentrating on the cricket. A few seconds later, the creature was standing before him, smiling kindly.

"I have come, Danny," he said.

"Thank you, Argill. It's Lucy, she's hurt and we can't help her," Danny said worriedly.

Argill patted his arm. "Let's see what we can do."

Some time later, Lucy was sitting up by the fire, her face pale and drawn. The wound on her arm had stopped bleeding and she was no longer in any pain. Argill was busy explaining to the cavewomen which herbs he had used to treat her. As soon as he had finished, he took Danny quietly to one side.

"I was wondering why you didn't help Lucy," he said in his soft voice.

"I did try, Argill, but I couldn't do it, no matter how hard I concentrated," Danny replied.

"Really? That's very strange, there is no reason why you shouldn't have been able to heal her," Argill said, thinking. He caught sight of Danny glancing over at Lucy. "Very well, we will speak again later. I can see you are impatient to go and see Lucy now and I know she wants to see you."

83

Lucy smiled weakly at Danny as he sat beside her. "I'm sorry, I could have prevented this. I was so proud of my stupid ropes, and making Tom walk all the way back here, but I didn't even think of getting rid of the wild beasts. It's all my fault you got hurt."

"It's OK, I'm fine now," Lucy replied. "It was pretty scary, though. I really thought I was a goner for a moment! I think I'd rather go in the Dark Forest than do that again." She laughed and squeezed Danny's hand. "Let's hope they move soon, it's too risky for them to stay here."

"Yeah, we didn't see any dangerous animals on the other side of the waterfall," Danny agreed. "Maybe they prefer to stay here close to the wood, where there are more places to hide. Well, I've got to go and speak with the wise men, tell them we've found their new home."

"Good luck," Lucy said. "Do you want me to come with you for moral support?"

"No, you stay here and rest. There shouldn't be any problems, I think they'll be very happy with what we found."

The wise men greeted Danny warmly, congratulating him on his successful journey and sympathising with Lucy's accident.

"We have found an enormous cave at the foot of a mountain, where there's lots of space for all of you to live and miles of underground tunnels for you to hide in if you are ever attacked," Danny explained. "It's close to a river teeming with fish, there are plenty of animals for you to hunt, and the ground is covered with lots of fruit bushes and even wild corn you can learn to cultivate."

"What's corn?" one of the wise men asked.

"A grain you can make into all sorts of wonderful foods. You'll soon learn how to use it, don't worry."

The wise men nodded appreciatively. "We hope you and your friends will stay for one last meal, and allow us to thank you for all your help."

"We'd love to!" Danny exclaimed. He returned to the others and told them the good news.

Tom patted his stomach in anticipation. "I can't wait!"

Lucy groaned. "Don't you ever think about anything else?" Just then a delicious aroma of roasted meat and herbs wafted over to them. "Mind you, I'm starting to feel hungry again, too," she laughed.

The sound of giggling came from behind them. Danny turned to see Ramda and Urdi, Totom's children, standing shyly to one side.

"We have present," they said quietly and held a parcel out to him.

"Thank you," he said solemnly, taking the gift. Wrapped up in a piece of animal hide were two long, sharp fangs that looked very familiar to him, tied to a long cord.

"They keep away evil spirits," Totom said, walking over to them. "You wear teeth, they protect you."

"I will, thank you," Danny replied. "Tom, will you keep them safe for me? I'll definitely need to wear them during our adventures here in Dreamland!"Tom carefully took the fangs and put them into a pouch he always wore around his neck. "Now," he said, rubbing his hands together in anticipation, "I do believe there's a feast waiting to be eaten!"

The three friends ate to their hearts' content, recounting their adventures over and over again as more cavemen came to listen. Danny was in the middle of telling a group of wide-eyed children all about the animal attack when he felt a familiar tugging sensation and noticed everything around him slowly dissolving. Tom and Lucy raised their hands to wave goodbye, and then everything turned grey and misty until he opened his eyes and found himself lying in his bed. For just a moment he could still smell the delicious feast and hear the children's voices, then everything disappeared and he was in his bedroom, sunlight streaming through the windows and his mother's voice calling him for breakfast.

"Let's hope Okram keeps you safe in your new home," Danny murmured, as he began to get ready for school.

Chapter Seven
Bad Dreams

Danny and his best friend, Mike, sat fidgeting on the sofa while their mums drank coffee and chattered amiably. Mike poked Danny in the side, making him giggle. Danny's mum glanced at them.

"Why don't you two go to the tree house? Help yourselves to something to eat in the kitchen, if you want."

"Thanks, Mum," Danny said, as they ran out of the living room.

They walked down the garden to the tree house, Danny with his laptop tucked under his arm and Mike carrying their afternoon snack. They clambered up the ladder and through the trapdoor, glad to be back in their private den. After helping themselves to fizzy drinks and opening a packet of biscuits, they flopped down on the cushions scattered on the floor.

"It was a really great holiday, Mike!" Danny exclaimed, his mouth full of biscuit. "I've never been on a plane before. It was really cool seeing all the houses and cars below us, they looked so small. The food was pretty awful, though! Switzerland was incredible… we could see the lake from our hotel window and there were mountains everywhere. Look!"

One by one he showed Mike the photos, and told him all about his summer holiday with his mum and aunt. "We went walking in the mountains every day and Mum had a book so we could recognise the flowers and animals. We always had to take jumpers with us even though it was July, 'cos the weather could change just like that," he clicked his fingers. "It started raining one day, but luckily we found a bar just in time, it really poured down. We had a cup of hot chocolate and sat by a fire watching the storm. That was one of the best days," he added with a grin.

"Sounds great!" Mike said. "Look at the sky in these photos, it's really blue and clear. And the mountains, they've got snow on them even in the middle of summer!"

"Yeah, you've never seen anything like it, Mike," Danny replied. "Everything was so clear and clean, it looked like it had just been painted. I wanted to go up to the snow, but Mum said it was too far. But we might go back this winter to learn to ski. Aunty Lisa said she'd like to try."

The two boys talked and played all afternoon, pretending to be climbers scaling treacherous mountains. Mike was just about to rescue Danny, who had fallen down a deep crevice during an avalanche, when his mother arrived.

"Time to go home, Mike," she called.

"Oh, Mum, can't I stay a bit longer," Mike shouted, pulling Danny out from under a huge pile of cushions.

"'Fraid not, it's tea time," she called back. "You can come again another day."

The two boys slowly climbed down the ladder and made their way back to Danny's house.

"See you, Danny."

"Bye, Mike."

They waved goodbye to each other and Danny went indoors.

"Did Mike like the photos?" his mum asked.

"Yes, he did," Danny replied. "He said we must have had a great time."

"Well, we did, didn't we?" His mum gave him a hug. "I've prepared you a special treat for after dinner." Danny raised his eyebrows questioningly. "Hot chocolate," she laughed.

"Wow. Thanks, Mum. You're the greatest!" Danny said, kissing her on the cheek.

Later that evening, the two of them were looking through the photos one last time.

"Mum, I wish we could live in the mountains," Danny said wistfully.

"You might not be so keen in winter, Danny. It snows a lot and it's always freezing cold, I don't think you'd find it that much fun!"

"I just feel, I don't know... like I belong there," Danny replied. His mum looked at him strangely, tears in her eyes.

"Your dad loved the mountains, Danny," she murmured. "We used to go skiing every winter, before you were born." Danny didn't say anything. They rarely spoke about his dad and he wasn't sure he wanted to now. His mum shook her head and smiled at him.

"That's enough for tonight. Bed now," and she shooed him up the stairs. Danny quickly got ready for bed and picked a book off his bookshelf to read.

"Have you put your ticket under your pillow?" his mum asked while tucking him into bed.

"No, it's in my bedside table drawer," Danny answered, avoiding her gaze. She took hold of his chin and turned his face towards her.

"Why's that, Danny?" she said gently.

"Oh, you know… I don't go *every* night," he mumbled.

"But you haven't been since we went on holiday. Your friends will be wondering where you are." She opened the drawer and pulled out the familiar silver ticket. Danny took it in his hand and looked at it. "Is something wrong, Danny?"

"No, of course not. You're right, Tom and Lucy will be waiting for me." He put the ticket under his pillow and smiled. His mum kissed him goodnight and closed his bedroom door.

Danny lay down, but didn't fall asleep straight away as he usually did. He looked up at the bedroom ceiling, thoughts racing through his mind. To be honest, he was scared to go back to Dreamland. Since Lucy's encounter with the wild animal, several other adventures had taken an unpleasant turn. He shuddered as he recalled an adventure they had had together just before he left for Switzerland…

They were racing through the desert on their camels, swaying from side to side as the animals lumbered across the sands. The hot desert sun beat down unmercifully on them, the featureless landscape shimmering hazily in the distance. Licking his dry, cracked lips and leaning closer to his camel to protect his eyes from the dusty air, he glanced back and saw that Tom and Lucy were far behind, shouting at their camels as they desperately tried to catch up with him. Looking ahead again, he noticed that his camel was approaching a particularly high sand dune. He gripped tightly with his legs as it lurched up the slope, praying that he could get up it without falling off.

As the animal reached the top, Danny's eyes widened in fear as a strange, shadowy figure slowly floated over the crest of the dune. Then the camel stumbled slightly and Danny hastily clutched onto the reins. He felt the sands shift beneath the animal, and the two of them rolled down the other side of the dune, over and over, until they landed in a heap at the bottom. Danny was trapped underneath the camel, sand filling his mouth and nose, suffocating him and making him panic. As he lay buried, he thought he could hear a sinister, chuckling sound from close by. He'd woken up in his bed, kicking and thrashing his arms about, terrified…

It had taken him a long time to go back to sleep that night, and he had often thought about the eerie silhouette he had seen. He hadn't been back to Dreamland since, using the fact that he was on holiday as an excuse, but had to admit that he was anxious to see Tom and Lucy again.

"It's only a dream, what's the worst that can happen?" he said to himself. "After all, Argill is there to help me if I need him."

He started to relax, his eyes gradually growing heavier. The now-familiar grey mist enveloped him, cushioning his fall into Dreamland. Danny smiled as confused images began to fly around him, then suddenly everything went dark. He stiffened as he felt himself falling faster and faster through the nothingness, the wind whooshing past him, and he began to feel afraid. Spine-chilling laughter echoed around his ears, making his hair stand on end, and he heard a strange, clanking sound. Panic rose in his throat and he found it difficult to breathe. Several times he felt something brush past him, although he couldn't see anything there.

All of a sudden, a light appeared far below him which gradually grew brighter as he plummeted towards it. He concentrated on it with all his might, willing it to chase away the darkness that surrounded him. Then his descent slowed abruptly as he found himself bathed in bright sunlight and he landed gently on the ground. Looking up, he could see no sign of the blackness he had just fallen through. Heaving a sigh of relief, he wiped the sweat from his brow.

"Danny!" Two familiar faces appeared before him, grinning broadly.

"Tom! Lucy!" Danny had never been so pleased to see them.

"We were wondering where you'd got to," Lucy said. "You haven't been here for ages. We thought something had happened to you."

"I've been on holiday and I didn't take the ticket with me. I forgot to tell you I was going," Danny said. Then his face became serious. "Something *did* happen on the way here, though." He told them all about his fall into Dreamland.

"You must speak to Argill," Tom said, worriedly. "I've never heard of anything like that happening before."

"Oh, it's OK, Tom. It's probably nothing," Danny replied. But the gnome insisted that Danny speak with the cricket.

Argill's face grew serious as Danny gave him an account of his journey into Dreamland. "I have noticed several incidents during your last few trips here, Danny, in particular the last time during the camel race."

Tom and Lucy stared curiously as Danny's mouth dropped open in amazement. "You know all about that?" he whispered.

"I know everything that happens here, Danny. Usually I do not interfere, except when you call for me, but I would never let anything terrible happen. You may carry on with your adventures in total safety. Just don't go anywhere near the Dark Forest, that is the one place where I cannot help you easily."

"What do you think is happening, Argill?" Danny asked.

"An unpleasant character has entered Dreamland. I am trying to find out how and why, in the meantime, keep your wits about you and be careful. And enjoy yourselves," he added, laughing at the three worried faces staring at him. "Everything will be fine. I believe you will be climbing mountains tonight." He pointed over their shoulders.

Danny turned to see an enormous mountain range in the distance. "This should be fun!" he exclaimed. "Let's go!"

"That's the spirit, Danny," Argill said, watching them head towards their next adventure.

They stood in a beautiful valley with mountains towering over them on either side. Thick forests of pine trees covered the lower slopes, giving way to sheer granite rock faces covered in snow further up. The sun glinted off brilliant white glaciers, forcing them to shield their eyes from its brightness. A river flowed down from a nearby mountain and hurried past them, crystal-clear icy water rushing over large rocks that had fallen down from the crags above. Tawny-coloured cows grazed quietly in grassy meadows, the bells around their necks clanging as they moved. A dirt track on their right led to the nearest mountain, disappearing behind several ridges at its base.

"Wow," Lucy sighed, "this is fantastic! Look, can you see that church spire sticking out just above that ridge over there? Shall we go and take a look?"

"Perhaps there's a village," Tom suggested. "We could go and get some food to take with us."

"If there's a church, then there must be a village," Danny agreed. "Trust you to think about food, Tom, but I s'pose it's a good idea, we can have a picnic up in the mountain."

They made their way over to the ridge, gazing in awe at the breath-taking scenery around them. It took them some time to follow the path that wound among huge boulders strewn across the valley floor, but at last they reached the ridge.

"It's very quiet," Danny remarked.

Indeed, they couldn't hear any of the noises you would expect to hear from a village. No children's voices or dogs barking could be heard, no adults shouting across the street to each other, not even a radio turned up too loudly. They turned the final corner and looked around eagerly.

Lucy gasped in shock. "Oh no!"

They all stared open-mouthed in horror. The village lay nestled snugly against the mountainside, the houses fanning out from the church at its centre. But the once-picturesque wooden chalets were now mere burnt and blackened shells, their windows shattered as if from a mighty explosion. The charred remains of abandoned children's playthings were the only evidence that people had ever lived there.

"What's happened? Where's everyone gone?" Danny asked. "I wonder if the village has been abandoned a long time."

Tom sniffed the air. "The smell of smoke is still very strong, it must have happened very recently. I don't understand what could have destroyed a whole village like this."

They walked past the houses, calling out every now and then in the hope of finding someone who could explain what had happened, but they only came across more scenes of destruction. They finally arrived at a barn resting in the shadow of the mountain, its blackened rafters reaching towards the sky. Several goats gazed nonchalantly at them, wisps of straw hanging from their mouths. The road through the village ended abruptly just after the barn, at the side of the mountain. Tom, Lucy and Danny looked at each other helplessly.

"Shall we go back?" Danny asked. The others shrugged their shoulders.

"Maybe we can look for the villagers further up the valley," Tom suggested. They remained in silence for a while, unsure what to do next.

"What's that noise?" Lucy said suddenly. They all listened carefully. They could hear a sobbing noise coming from somewhere nearby.

"There, in the barn," Tom whispered. They moved closer.

"Hello," Danny called. "Who's there?" There was no reply, but the crying grew louder.

"We're not going to hurt you," Lucy said, "we just want to help. Where are you?"

The sobbing ceased and a few moments later a little girl's small, grubby face peeped around the barn door. She stared at them, twisting a lock of her long, black hair around her finger, her green eyes wide open and filled with fear.

"Hello," Lucy said gently. "Why don't you come out here and tell us who you are?"

The child looked nervously up at the sky, then shook her head.

"Can we come in there, then?" Lucy asked. The girl nodded. "Poor thing, she can only be five or six years old," Lucy whispered to the others.

They went into the barn. The girl looked out at them from under a fallen beam and motioned to them to sit beside her.

"I'm Lucy, this is Tom, and this is Danny," Lucy said, when they were all squashed together. "What's your name?"

"Malia," the girl replied, sniffing.

"What happened here, Malia?" Danny asked.

The girl stared at them. "You didn't see it? It's gone?"

"There's nothing outside now," Danny replied. "What did you see?"

The girl's lip wobbled and tears filled her eyes. "A d-dragon."

"What?" they exclaimed.

"It flew out of the sky, breathing fire. It burnt all the houses and everyone ran away. I came in here to hide and I called for my mummy and daddy, but… no one came." She broke into loud, heaving sobs and Lucy put her arm around her.

"When did the dragon come?" Tom asked.

"Just after breakfast, I think. I've been here for ages on my own. I just want my mummy." She leant against Lucy's shoulder, sucking her thumb.

"Why would the dragon attack the village?" Danny asked the others.

Tom shrugged. "If there *was* a dragon," he muttered.

"What else could have done all that damage?" Lucy asked. "Don't you believe her, Tom?"

The gnome scowled. "She's only a little kid," he said stubbornly.

"There are lots of stories about the dragon," Malia piped up. "Daddy told me that he used to attack all the villages in the valley, until he made a pact with King Marcus. In return for all the king's gold he promised to stay up in the mountain, away from us. As long as no one touches the treasure, he leaves the villages in the valley in peace. He lives in a cave high up in the mountain, where he has been sleeping for five hundred years on a bed of gold and precious stones. Many have climbed the mountain to kill the dragon and steal his treasure, but no one has ever managed to find his lair."

"So why did he attack?" Tom asked.

The girl remained silent for a while, then suddenly stood up and ran out of the barn. After a few minutes she returned, carrying a heavy object. She handed it solemnly to Lucy, tears in her eyes.

"I found it by the stream yesterday, when I went there to play. It was lying in the water. I think this may be what he was looking for." She started crying again.

"It was so pretty, I wanted to keep it and pretend I was a princess. I didn't th-think it belonged to the d-dragon."

Lucy handed her a tissue. Danny and Tom looked at the object she was holding. It was an ornate, golden crown, richly decorated with rubies and sapphires. Tom whistled.

"I can understand why the dragon's upset, this is really valuable," he said.

"We have to get it back to him, then he won't attack any of the other villages in the valley," Danny said.

"And where do we look for him?" Tom asked. "No one's found his cave in five hundred years!"

"Well, we have to go higher up the mountain, so perhaps we should follow the stream," Danny replied. "It's possible the crown fell in the water when the dragon went to drink, so we might find his lair near the water. Malia, will you show us where you found it, please?"

The girl looked at him in surprise. "Me?"

"Yes, if you're not too scared to come with us," Danny said. "I promise you the dragon is nowhere around now."

They all left the barn, Danny carrying the crown inside his jacket. Malia led the way through the village, all fear gone now that she had other people with her. The three friends kept an eye out for the dragon, but there was no sign of it anywhere.

"Here's where I found the crown," Malia cried when they arrived at a bend in the stream.

Danny looked around. "Now we'll follow the stream up the mountain and hopefully we'll eventually find the cave," he said.

"Great plan," Tom muttered, glancing up at the mountain. "How far will we have to go?"

"I really don't know," Danny replied, "but the sooner we start, the quicker we'll get there!"

The climb was pleasant at first. They followed the meandering stream up gentle slopes and through flowery meadows full of cows chewing the cud and shy rabbits that disappeared in a flash of bobbing white tails as the friends drew near. Danny, Tom, and Lucy gasped in delight as a herd of deer ran past them across a grassy field and vanished among the fir trees. Malia pointed out all the wild animals to them.

After a while they followed the stream into a dense pine forest and it became more difficult for them to make progress. They stopped talking as they pushed their way through the trees, their arms and faces getting scratched by sharp pine needles. The slopes became steadily steeper and covered in small stones, making them slip, and soon their knees were sore and bleeding. It was hard work climbing through the forest and they were all starting to get tired and fed up.

Eventually they stopped to sit by a fallen tree for a rest, leaning back against its trunk. Malia immediately fell asleep with her head on Lucy's knee, snoring gently. Lucy looked around wearily, wondering how much further they had to go.

"Look over there, on that rock in the middle of the stream," she said softly, careful not to wake Malia. Danny and Tom tiredly raised their heads and saw that there was a small, gold object on the rock.

Danny waded into the water and picked it up. "It's a ring!" he cried. "We must be getting closer."

Malia stirred and sat up. "What's that you've got?" she asked, yawning.

Danny showed her the ring. "Look, it has the same pattern as the crown, it must be some more of the dragon's treasure. We're on the right track!"

"So does this mean we're going to carry on?" Lucy asked.

"Of course, but let's hope it's not too far now," Danny replied.

The trees got thicker and thicker, making it harder to follow the stream, and the air began to grow much colder. All of a sudden, they burst through some branches and found themselves on the very edge of the pine forest. Ahead, the tips of huge, granite boulders jutted out of a vast expanse of snow and they could just make out the mountain peak way above them.

"Gosh, it's cold," Tom shivered. "Can't you get us some coats, please, Danny?"

Danny grinned and closed his eyes. Within seconds they were all wearing warm, padded coats, gloves, scarves and hats.

"That's better!" the gnome said, flapping his arms.

Lucy ran off and collected a handful of snow and Tom spluttered as a snowball hit him in the face. Danny and Malia burst out laughing, and soon snowballs were whizzing through the air in all directions. Eventually they all collapsed on the ground, gasping for breath.

"Feels a bit warmer now, doesn't it, Tom?" Lucy said, standing up and brushing snow from her clothes. She giggled at Tom's bedraggled appearance. The gnome snorted angrily and stomped away from her.He bent over to do up his shoelace, then suddenly turned around and threw an enormous snowball right in Lucy's face. She fell over backwards, spluttering crossly.

"Now we're even," he said, grinning at her.

"Sssh, you two," Danny said suddenly.

"What's wrong, Danny?" Lucy asked.

"Can you see smoke?"

They all stopped messing around and looked to where he was pointing. To their right was an enormous rock protruding from the mountainside and two grey columns of smoke were clearly visible above it, rising into the air.

"You three stay here," Danny whispered. Tom began to object, but fell silent at the look on Danny's face. "If anything happens, run back to the forest and hide. Take care of Malia," he added, noticing that the little girl's face was white with fear. Tom and Lucy nodded, their hearts in their mouths as they watched Danny walk towards the outcrop of rock.

Chapter Eight
Dragons And Sorcery

Danny peered around the edge of the rock, his heart beating wildly. There in the mouth of a dank, cold cavern was an enormous dragon curled up like a sleeping dog, its long body disappearing into the dark recesses of the cave. Two long, leathery wings were tucked close against its sides and a long, serpentine tail snaked back across the cave floor. Its body was covered in green and gold scales and a ridge of jagged spines ran the length of its back, from head to tail. A huge, scaly head rested on its front legs and fearsome, curved claws slowly scratched deep grooves in the loose earth. It had a long, pointed spike on the end of its nose and spiny horns on either side of each ear, and two spirals of smoke rose languidly from its dark nostrils.

Danny breathed in sharply - the dragon's claws were *moving*. Perhaps it wasn't really asleep! Just then, the creature opened its red eyes and glared malevolently at him. It clambered laboriously to its feet, grunting, and stretched its immense, bat-like wings. Danny could see the whole of its body now: the armour-plated underbelly, the barbed tip of its coiled tail, and a wicked-looking sharp spur on each of its chunky legs. Large pieces of gold were embedded in its scaly hide and treasure lay scattered all around the cave floor.

"You don't look much like a dragon slayer to me," the dragon said lazily in a deep, rumbling voice. "More like a dragon supper. Ha, ha, ha." His mouth opened wide, showing row upon row of enormous, razor-sharp fangs. Danny shivered; the dragon's laugh was hollow and empty-sounding, completely bereft of humour. "Luckily for you, I've just eaten," he continued, scraping at his teeth with a claw. "So speak, boy, tell me why you are here."

Danny gulped. "I-I would like to know why you attacked the village and wh-where all the people have gone."

"I attacked the village because someone stole a precious piece of treasure from me," the dragon roared, making Danny jump. "The villagers ran away when they saw me coming. I don't know where they've gone, but I'll make sure they won't come back." He snorted in anger, a long flame of fire shooting out from his nose. Danny leapt back in fright. Recovering himself, he approached the dragon again.

"Did you lose a crown, by any chance?" he asked the creature.

"How do you know that?" the dragon said suspiciously. "Did *you* steal it?"

"No, no! A girl from the village found it, by the stream."

"I went to the stream a few days ago. There was a herd of wild goats there, drinking… I ate well that day."

Danny tried to hide his fear. "Perhaps you lost it at the stream," he suggested.

"I suppose that is possible. Where is the crown now?"

"I have it," Danny replied.

The dragon moved forward, a greedy expression on his face. "Give it to me, boy," he demanded.

Danny shook his head. "First you must promise not to harm me or my friends, and to leave all the villagers alone from now on."

"I haven't bothered anyone in five hundred years," the dragon growled angrily. "I only attacked yesterday because I thought someone had stolen my crown. It's very valuable, King Marcus gave it to me."

"Promise," Danny repeated.

"All right, I promise," the dragon said sulkily, stretching his long snout towards the boy.

Danny took the crown out of his jacket and placed it on the ground. He put his hand in his pocket and felt the ring he had found in the stream earlier on. He clasped it in his fist, then suddenly decided to hold on to it for a little while longer.

The dragon used his snout to nudge the crown to the back of the cave, then turned back to Danny. "So, boy, you have brought me my crown. That shows great courage on your part and I am in your debt. Tell me, how can I repay you?"

"First of all, you can call me Danny. What's your name?"

"I am Flameshooter. I apologise for scaring you earlier, I thought you had come to steal more of my treasure. I never imagined that you would be returning it to me! So tell me, Danny, how can I repay you?"

"Well, there is one thing you could do," Danny replied.

A little while later, Danny, Tom, Lucy, and Malia were clinging on to Flameshooter's scaly back for dear life, while the dragon flew high in the air. Far below them they could see the mountain range and the valley where their adventure had started. Lucy tapped Danny's shoulder and pointed down at Malia's village, where they could see people walking among the ruined houses. Danny was glad to see that the villagers were going back home and promised himself that he would make them brand new houses before the dream ended. The dragon began his descent, coming to land on an outcrop of rock on the mountain peak. Danny, Lucy, Tom, and Malia slithered off his back, happy to be on the ground once more.

"Why has the dragon taken us to the top of the mountain, Danny?" Lucy asked.

"I thought we might ski back down," Danny replied, laughing.

Tom groaned. "I was afraid you'd say that."

"Oh, come on, Tom, it'll be fun," Danny said. "We can all have a go, even Malia. I bet she's an expert already. Isn't that right, Malia?"

They turned towards her, their smiles turning to concern when they realised that she was nowhere to be seen.

"Malia!" Lucy called loudly. They all began shouting her name, wondering where she could be.

"She's probably hiding again," Tom said, trying not to sound worried. "She'll jump out in a minute, laughing her head off."

Danny nodded. "You're probably right, Tom."

"If you don't mind, I would like to go back to my cave," the dragon interrupted. "I don't like to be away from my treasure for too long. Besides, it has been hard work carrying the four of you to the top of the mountain and I am starting to feel hungry again." He yawned, his enormous, white fangs glistening in the sunlight.

"That's all right, Flameshooter," Danny said. "Thanks for the fantastic ride." He put his hand into his pocket, about to give the ring he had found in the stream back to the dragon. "I think this belongs…" he began, then stopped as Lucy screamed loudly.

Standing before them was a tall woman, the cold wind whipping her long, black hair about her pale face. Her bright green eyes glared venomously at them, filled with hatred. She would have been beautiful but for her thin, cruel, mouth and prominent cheekbones that were flushed red with fury. She was wearing a purple dress covered with a lacy cobweb pattern, and a fine gold chain around her waist. On her head was a black, pointed hat with a small, red snake coiled around the tip and in her hand was a wand, which she was pointing at them.

"Stregona!" Tom exclaimed fearfully.

"What?" Danny asked. "That's Stregona?"

"Yes," Lucy whispered.

"What have you done with Malia?" Danny shouted defiantly.

The witch glared at him. "Fool," she sneered haughtily. "I *am* Malia." She twisted her hair around her finger, and opened her eyes wide in mock fear. There was a moment of stunned silence as the three friends realised what she had just said.

"You're Malia?" Danny said finally. "Why did you deceive us?"

"To capture you, Danny," the witch replied with an evil laugh.

Flameshooter suddenly leapt to his feet, roaring with anger. Fire streamed from his mouth, aimed straight at Stregona. She lazily raised her wand in front of her and the flame vanished abruptly.

"You cannot destroy me with your fire, dragon," she said calmly.

"I will not let you take Danny," Flameshooter replied, panting. "He was brave enough to return my treasure to me and I will repay my debt."

"Idiot!" The witch's scornful voice rang out loud and clear in the crisp air. "It was all because of me that Danny came to you!"

"Explain, witch," the dragon rumbled.

"*I* stole your treasure because I knew that you would attack the villagers. Then I disguised myself as a girl and waited for Danny and his friends to show up. It was easy to convince them I had been left behind in the panic. I knew Danny would want to help the villagers by returning your treasure to you because he always wants to play the hero. Then I could use you to help me take Danny back to my house."

Flameshooter snorted furiously and lunged forward. The witch flicked her wand and he stopped, unable to move at all. Danny clenched his fists, feeling powerless to help the dragon.

Tom stared at her incredulously. "You planned all of this, just to catch Danny? Why? Why is Danny so important to you?"

"Oh, the boy means nothing to me," Stregona replied carelessly. "*He* wants Danny."

The hair on the back of Danny's neck prickled with fear.

"Who?" Tom insisted.

Lucy glanced at Danny's white face. "She's talking about the one who scared you while you fell into Dreamland tonight, isn't she?"

"Who is he?" Danny asked the witch, his voice trembling slightly.

"He is the most powerful wizard I have ever met," Stregona replied. "He wants you, Danny, and I have promised to take you to Him." She strode towards the dragon, muttering words in a strange language. Flameshooter's eyes shone briefly, then glazed over and his body sagged. Stregona took the gold chain from around her waist and placed it around his long, sinewy neck.

"Get on the dragon's back," she ordered.

Tom, Danny, and Lucy walked slowly over to the dragon, hand in hand.

"Call Argill," Tom whispered. As Danny closed his eyes, the witch pointed her wand at them and they all fell down in a heap on the snow, unconscious.

Danny groaned as he came to, his whole body aching. As his eyes began to focus, he noticed that he was lying on a dusty, wooden floor in a dimly lit house. He slowly sat up, trying not to jolt his throbbing head. He realised he was no longer wearing the heavy ski suit and wondered where it had gone.

"Tom, Lucy," he whispered nervously. A nearby shape stirred slightly.

"Danny?" came Lucy's voice. "Where are we?"

"Sssh, not too loud," Danny whispered. "Stregona might be around. She captured us, remember?" He reached over and held Lucy's hand.

"She wanted us to get on Flameshooter," Lucy said. "Then Tom told you to call Argill and… and I don't remember anything else."

"She must have cast a spell on us," Danny said. "She did something to Flameshooter when he refused to obey her."

"Yes, I remember now," Lucy replied. "Danny, why don't you try and call Argill now, while she's not around."

Danny closed his eyes and concentrated on the cricket, willing him to come and help them. Minutes passed but nothing happened. Danny and Lucy looked at each other in despair.

"'S'no good," said a muffled voice behind them. "We're in Stregona's house in the Dark Forest, Argill can't help us here."

"Tom!" they cried, flinging their arms around him.

Lucy burst into tears. "This is terrible. We're supposed to keep Danny out of trouble and take him on great adventures, and now look what's happened!" She sobbed helplessly, tears pouring down her cheeks.

"It's OK, Lucy," Danny said. "We've been in the Dark Forest before and got out all right. We just have to keep calm and see what happens."

Tom handed her a tissue. "Chin up, Lucy," he said gruffly. "Danny's right, we'll get out of this soon."

"That's the spirit, Tom," Danny said. "Now, shall we see if we can get out of this house?" They explored every inch of the room they were in, but could find no sign of a door or window. Danny even checked for a trapdoor in the floor, but found nothing.

"How did we get in here?" he wondered.

"By magic," Lucy said. "We can't get out unless Stregona frees us."

They sat huddled together on the floor against a wall. Danny traced the outline of a knot in the wood, then noticed a small gap between the planks of wood. He put his face close to the wall, trying to peer through, and felt cool, fresh air on his skin. "If only I had a knife," he muttered.

"Why's that?" Tom asked.

"There's a small hole in the wall here," Danny replied. "If I had a knife I could try to make it larger. At least then we could see where we are and maybe call for help."

Tom chuckled. "Do you remember our adventure with the cavemen?" He handed Danny the pouch from around his neck. "And the good luck charm they gave you?"

"Of course!" Danny exclaimed. "The sabre-toothed tiger's fangs!" He took one of the teeth out of the pouch and began using it to enlarge the small gap, wiggling it from side to side. Tom and Lucy watched him, holding their breath.

After a while, he stood back. "That will do for now," he said. He had made a hole about the size of a walnut.

Tom looked through it. "We're in a clearing in the Dark Forest," he said to the others. "There's not much light, but I can see Flameshooter. He's tied to some trees at the edge of the clearing, not too far away."

"Any sign of Stregona?" Lucy asked.

"Can't see her," the gnome replied. "But she could be anywhere."

"Maybe we can use Flameshooter to escape," Danny suggested.

"Only if we can break the spell he's under," Tom answered. He looked through the hole again. "Trolls!" he said suddenly.

They could hear the trolls talking nearby in a strange, guttural language, and then Stregona's voice rang out, speaking in the same language.

"Cover the hole," Danny whispered. Tom tore off a piece of his shirt and stuffed it into the hole. They all sat down, their hearts thumping wildly.

Suddenly there was a loud, cracking sound and a door appeared in the opposite wall. Stregona strode into the room, followed by two trolls.

"I see you are awake," she said, glaring at them. "I have sent some trolls to let Him know that I have caught you. He will be here soon, it should be an extraordinary meeting."

"All the more extraordinary as we won't be here," Danny replied, staring defiantly at the witch.

"Brave words, Danny," she sneered. "We shall see how brave you are when He arrives." She turned and left the room, the two trolls shuffling after her. The wall sealed shut again, leaving no trace of the door.

Danny tugged the piece of cloth out of the hole in the wall and began hacking furiously with the fang. Tom and Lucy watched in silence, anxiety etched on their faces. Suddenly the tooth snapped, leaving a deep cut in Danny's hand. He cried out, blood dripping from the wound.

"Here, let me have a look," Lucy said, wrapping a clean handkerchief around his hand.

"You have to be more careful." Tom gave him the second fang. "This is the last one, so don't break it. And try to be quiet," he added. "Stregona might have left trolls on guard."

Danny nodded and began enlarging the hole again, more carefully this time. After a while, he handed the fang to Tom. "You take over, I need to rest."

Tom carried on, the hole now as large as a melon.

"What if they see it?" Lucy asked Danny.

"That's a chance we'll have to take," he replied grimly. "We can't just sit here and wait."

Lucy took over from Tom, digging and tugging at the wood, praying that no one would see her. The hole was now large enough for her head to fit through and she had a clear view of what was going on outside. As she worked, she thought that she could see something moving through the trees to her left. She peered through the hole, trying to make out what it was, but there was not enough light for her to see by. Then she heard a loud, cracking noise, as if the trees' branches were being snapped from their trunks.

"Danny, I think something's happening," she said nervously. Danny crouched down beside her, looking through the hole. She squeezed his hand tightly.

"We won't let you come to any harm." Tom put his hand on Danny's shoulder.

Danny made a wry face, his throat too dry to speak. The cracking noise grew louder, now accompanied by a thundering that made the ground tremble. The three friends watched helplessly as several trees crashed to the ground, leaves and twigs flying into the air.

Trolls ran into the clearing, waving enormous clubs and shouting at each other. They advanced slowly towards the fallen trees, where the dust and debris was gradually settling. Then Stregona came into view, her dress flapping about her body in the breeze.

"What is the meaning of this?" she shouted.

Danny, Lucy, and Tom looked at each other, startled.

"It's obviously not *him* arriving," Danny whispered. "What's going on?"

The witch waved her hand imperiously at the trolls. Several of them took a few hesitant steps forward, reluctant to approach the trees. Suddenly an enormous pair of legs stepped through the gap. The trolls slowly raised their heads, their eyes travelling up the length of the mountainous body before them. Trembling, they ran back to the witch, cowering behind her.

"Cowards!" she shouted angrily. She turned to face the giant. "What do you want here?"

The giant bent down until his huge, round face filled the clearing.

"Grullo!" Tom, Lucy, and Danny shouted in delight, recognising him immediately.

"Answer me, giant," Stregona shouted.

A smile broke out on Grullo's face. "Grullo bring help for Danny," he boomed.

"What?" The witch raised her wand angrily. "I don't think so."

Just then, a shadowy figure moved out from behind the giant. "Put down your wand, Stregona," Argenta said firmly.

"Leave, unicorn, before you get hurt," Stregona replied.

Other unicorns stepped out from the trees, until the clearing was filled with the beautiful, pure-white creatures. "Give us Danny, Tom, and Lucy, and we shall leave," Argenta said.

Stregona turned to her trolls and said something to them. They immediately grasped hold of their clubs and began stomping their feet on the ground. The unicorns lowered their heads and charged. There was a moment's silence, and then the air was filled with yells, neighs and sickening, thudding noises as weapons found their marks.

Danny began to kick desperately at the wall, breaking the wood with his feet. "We've got to help them," he cried. Tom and Lucy started kicking as well and soon the wood gave way with a loud, splintering noise. They ran outside, then stopped abruptly as they saw Stregona striding towards Flameshooter.

"Danny!" cried a voice to their right. Danny turned and saw a handsome, young unicorn galloping towards them, his long, pearl-coloured horn fending off several trolls in his way. He came to a halt before them and tossed his flowing mane, neighing happily.

"*Joey*? Is that you?" Danny said. "What are you doing here?"

"Rescuing you," the unicorn replied cheekily. "Come on!"

"Wait," Danny said. "Stregona is going to use the dragon. We have to stop her."

"Are you crazy?" Joey yelled. "We have to get away from here."

"How?" Tom asked. "We're surrounded. There's no way out of the clearing."

Indeed, more trolls had poured into the clearing to join the fight. Grullo was using his great hands as clubs, throwing trolls left and right as he moved, but even more came to take the place of the ones that had fallen. Everywhere the three friends looked they could see a confusion of unicorns and trolls battling furiously.

"The dragon's our only hope," Danny yelled to the others. He began running towards the beast, Tom and Lucy following closely behind.

Flameshooter was lumbering to his feet just as Danny arrived, Stregona uttering magic words in his ear. Danny pulled the ring from his pocket and held it at arm's length, standing in front of the dragon.

"Flameshooter, it's me, Danny," he cried. "I have your ring. I found it in the stream on the way up the mountain. I brought you your crown, remember, and now I need your help!"

A spark appeared in Flameshooter's eyes and he shook his head, looking confused. "Danny?" he said uncertainly, trying to focus on the boy standing before him.

"Here's your ring, Flameshooter!" Danny cried, throwing it in the air. Flameshooter tossed his head and caught it on one of his horns.

"No!" Stregona shouted, raising her wand. She opened her mouth to say the spell, but it was too late. Flameshooter let out a terrible roar and tugged on the chains tying him to the trees, snapping them easily. He shook his head and sent the witch's gold chain flying across the clearing, where it was soon trampled underfoot by the battling trolls and unicorns.

Swinging his tail around, he whipped the wand from Stregona's hand, throwing it far into the forest. Flames of fire poured from his mouth, setting several trees ablaze. As his roar echoed through the clearing, the trolls, unicorns and giant ceased their fighting. Everyone turned to where Stregona and the dragon faced each other.

"Come Danny, Tom, and Lucy," Flameshooter said with a rumbling growl. They walked past Stregona, not daring to look at her, and climbed onto his back.

"You will leave Danny and his friends alone, witch," the dragon said angrily. "And you can tell your 'friend', whoever he is, that the unicorns, giants and dragons will protect Danny, should he try anything like this again."

"You will regret the day you opposed His will," Stregona said in an evil tone. "He is mightier than all of you." She looked around at everyone in the clearing. "Be gone with you, miserable creatures," she shouted at the trolls, walking back towards her house.

Flameshooter soared into the sky, heading for Dreamland. Looking back, Danny saw trees bending and shaking as Grullo and the unicorns made their way to the edge of the forest. Feeling safe at last, he leaned forward and rested his head against the dragon's neck. He pictured the ruined village in his mind and concentrated on making the buildings whole again.

Opening his eyes, he saw that they were coming to land once more in the valley they had started out from. He could hear a church bell ringing joyfully and the sound of people cheering happily.

"At least some good came out of tonight's adventure," he murmured, as the dragon landed smoothly on the ground.

Argill was waiting for them as Flameshooter came to a halt. "I am so sorry, Danny," he said as they slid off the dragon's back. "I have been searching all of Dreamland for this intruder and didn't see what was happening on the mountain until it was too late. Thank you, Flameshooter, for saving Danny, Tom, and Lucy," he added, bowing low.

The dragon lowered its head. "I am grateful that Danny managed to break Stregona's spell. How did you know what to do, Danny?"

"I didn't. I found the ring in a stream and decided to keep it in case I needed it later on. I think Stregona left it there for me to find, to convince me we were on the right track."

"Why didn't she take it from you?" Flameshooter asked.

Danny shrugged, baffled.

"She probably thought you gave it back to Flameshooter together with the crown and didn't realise you still had it," Lucy said.

Flameshooter snorted. "It's lucky for you that we dragons are so jealous of our treasure, it was probably the only way to break Stregona's spell!"

119

They all burst out laughing, glad to break the tension for a moment. Then the dragon became serious again. "These are bad times in Dreamland," he said gravely. "Have you found out who Stregona was helping, Argill?"

The cricket sighed. "I'm afraid so."

"Well?" Tom said impatiently. "Who is he? How can we fight him?"

Argill looked at Danny sadly. "You have brought him to Dreamland."

"Me? How?" Danny cried. "I would never do anything to hurt anyone here, you know that."

"I know, Danny. It was not done willingly, or even knowingly, but you have allowed this being into Dreamland." Argill put a hand on Danny's shoulder. "His name is Incubus and he comes from your subconscious. You have something hidden deep within you, Danny, which is manifesting itself here in Dreamland. If you let it, it will continue to grow and eat away at you until you have no spirit left."

"If I let it," Danny repeated in a subdued tone.

"You have two choices," Argill said. "You can awake now, throw away your ticket and never return here again. Incubus will leave us alone and we will be safe, but he will still be inside you, waiting to strike when you least expect it. Or you can return to Dreamland, confront Incubus and, with the help of all your friends here, overcome him and destroy him once and for all."

Danny stood in silence, thinking. All of a sudden he heard the sound of hooves galloping up behind him, and then something bumped into his bottom.

"What the...?" he began, and then laughed. "Oh, it's you, Joey. Look at you, all grown up!"

"Yeah, thanks for using your imagination to make me grow up so quickly," the unicorn laughed. "You must have known I'd be more use to you like this!" Then he began leaping about, darting from one person to the other. "Tom, Lucy, tell Danny we'll all be here to help him and that he has to come back." He looked beseechingly at the group of friends.

"How can we refuse?" Lucy giggled.

Tom grinned broadly and patted Joey's head. "I'll be here, don't worry."

Flameshooter frowned at the unicorn, who skipped neatly out of the dragon's way. "I'll be here, if you stop dancing around. You're making my head spin," he growled. "Otherwise I might have to eat you up and use your horn as a toothpick!" His face was stern but his eyes were twinkling in amusement.

Joey leapt back in fright and crashed into his mother.

"Are you getting into trouble again, Joey?" Argenta sighed.

"No, Mum, I was just asking everyone to help Danny, and *he* said he'd eat me and use my horn as a toothpick. Unlike others, *I* would defend Danny with my life." The young unicorn glowered at Flameshooter from the safety of his mother's side.

121

"It's all right, Joey, I'm sure Flameshooter was just joking," Argenta soothed, winking at the dragon. "Your horn would be far too small for him to use as a toothpick!"

"My apologies," Flameshooter growled, with a hint of a smile on his enormous mouth. "I did not realise that I was speaking to Danny's most loyal companion." He lowered his face until it was close to Joey's. "I am forever at your service, my friend," he said, bowing low.

"Well, Danny, it looks like we'll all be here to help you!" Joey exclaimed happily.

Danny looked around at all of his friends, tears in his eyes. "All of you?" he asked.

They nodded. Lucy took his hand in hers. "Please come back again," she whispered.

"It won't be easy, Danny, and it could even be dangerous," Argill warned. "Incubus is getting more and more powerful every time you come back and he is plotting with Stregona and every other evil creature that lives in the Dark Forest. You should return as soon as possible if you wish to defeat him before he gets too strong. You must trust all of your friends here, especially Tom and Lucy. In the end, you will have to show them what you have kept hidden for so long."

Danny nodded. "I-I think I understand." He gave Tom and Lucy a big hug, then shook Argill's hand. "I will come back tomorrow night," he promised, stroking Joey's nose. "To defeat Incubus."

Chapter Nine
Saving Dreamland

The alarm clock beeped noisily, waking Danny up with a jolt. He reached out to turn it off and lay back down, relishing his last few moments in bed. He thought back to the previous night's adventure in the mountains, frowning as he remembered how Stregona had managed to deceive them. His mother's voice interrupted his thoughts as she called him down for his breakfast.

A few minutes later he appeared in the kitchen, yawning tiredly. His mother glanced at his pale face as he sat down at the breakfast table.

"Are you all right?" she asked.

"I'm OK, Mum, I just didn't sleep very well," he mumbled.

"You look a bit under the weather, I hope you're not coming down with something." She handed him his bowl of cereal and poured him a glass of orange juice.

"I'm fine," Danny answered, his mouth full of cereal. "I've got a project to finish for school and I'm a bit stressed about it."

His mum nodded, taking a sip of her coffee. "What's it about. I can give you a hand this afternoon if you want."

Danny took a mouthful of orange juice while desperately trying to think of a topic. "It's on medieval castles," he said hurriedly.

"I'll have a look for some books," his mum said. "Maybe I'll pop in to the library later and see if I can find anything."

"Thanks, Mum," Danny replied, feeling a little guilty. "Well, I guess I'd better get off to school, then." He gulped down the rest of his juice, pushed his chair under the table and picked up his school bag. "Bye, Mum," he called as he ran out of the door.

Danny found it hard to concentrate at school that day and he was glad when the going home bell finally rang. After telling his mum about his day, he went down the garden to his tree house. He flung himself down on some cushions, munching on an apple. Thoughts raced through his head as he tried to imagine how that night's visit to Dreamland would go. He hoped that Tom and Lucy would be waiting for him as usual, ready to share the adventure as they always did. He wondered if Argill and the unicorns would be there; he would even be happy to see Grullo. Not once did it occur to him not to go. It was his fault that Dreamland was in danger and he would be the one to save it, no matter what it cost him. He stayed in the tree house until dinnertime, making plans and going over all sorts of fantastic scenarios in his head.

Later that evening he ate his dinner slowly, savouring every mouthful. He and his mum talked about normal, everyday things, such as school, Mike, sport, girlfriends…

"*Mum*," Danny spluttered in horror. "I'm not interested in *girls*. They're OK as mates, but that's about it!"

"There must be someone you like, Danny," his mum teased.

"Ugh!" he said crossly, poking his tongue out. "If I had a girlfriend, I'd have to play dolls with her. Gross!"

His mum laughed at the disgusted expression on his face. "Oh, Danny, you'll soon change your mind."

"Never," Danny stated firmly. "Not in a million years."

All too soon, it was time for bed. His mum kissed him goodnight. "Tomorrow's Saturday, have a lie-in," she said. "Then we can have a look at those books I got from the library this afternoon."

"OK, Mum," Danny said sleepily. As she turned the light off, he reached under his pillow to see if the ticket was there. He held it in his hand a moment, rubbing his fingers over the black lettering, and then he put it carefully back in place. With a deep sigh, he closed his eyes and fell fast asleep.

His fall into Dreamland was uneventful this time. The swirling, grey mist cushioned his descent as usual, while indistinct shapes floated around him. Just once he thought he heard a sinister laugh, but he couldn't see anything in the darkness.

He landed gently on the ground and immediately looked all around, tense and alert. He was standing in the fairground again, but this time it was deserted. Pieces of paper rolled along the road, blown by the wind, and the rides creaked eerily. All the brightly coloured stalls were boarded up and he couldn't see any sign of people anywhere. A sudden loud noise made him jump; turning, he saw an empty drink can rattling along the ground towards him. His heart thumping, he picked it up and placed it in a nearby litter bin.

"Glad to see you're keeping Dreamland tidy, Danny," said a voice behind him.

"Argill!" Danny was pleased to see the cricket. "Where is everyone?"

"I've sent them all to other Dreamlands for now, where they will be safe," Argill replied.

"Oh," Danny said, disappointed. "Does that mean I'll be alone tonight?"

"Not everyone wanted to go."

Danny heard footsteps echoing on the road and suddenly Tom and Lucy burst into view. Lucy flung her arms around Danny and hugged him tightly, while Tom ruffled his hair.

"You didn't really think we'd leave you to fight Incubus alone, did you?" he teased.

Danny shook his head, too happy to speak.

"You have many friends here, Danny," Argill said. "You only have to call and they will come and help you." Then he became serious. "Do you remember what I said to you yesterday, about sharing your troubles?" he asked.

"Yes," Danny answered. "I–I think I'm ready."

"Not yet, Danny. You will know when it is time. First we must wait and see what surprises Incubus has in store for you. Stay alert, not everything will be as it seems. But remember to trust each other at all times... Incubus cannot destroy your friendship unless you let him."

"Aren't you coming with us," Danny asked worriedly.

"I cannot, Danny. It is forbidden for me to interfere in your adventures, except in cases of extreme need. But you can always call for me."

"*If* I am in danger," Danny replied gloomily.

Argill drew himself up to his full height. "This is your battle, Danny, I cannot fight Incubus for you. However," he added more kindly, "I *can* give you this."

He took a small metal flask out of his waistcoat pocket and handed it to Danny. It felt warm to the touch and the metal had soft, rainbow-coloured streaks in it. An ornate, silver sword with a snake entwined around the blade decorated the front of the flask and a long, silver chain was fastened to it. Danny passed the chain over his head so that the bottle rested on his chest.

"What is it?" he murmured.

"If you drink just one drop of this potion, for a few seconds you will be able to see whoever is standing before you in their true form," Argill told him.

"It would have been handy yesterday with Stregona," Tom remarked.

"Indeed," said the cricket. "But use it sparingly, there is only enough for you to use three or four times."

"Thank you Argill." Danny tucked the flask under his shirt. "I really appreciate all your help."

The cricket smiled and patted Danny's shoulder. "Be strong, Danny, and everything will work out for the best."

Danny took a deep breath and turned to Tom and Lucy. "Ready, then?" he asked.

The three friends began walking through the deserted fairground.

"By the way," Argill called, "the unicorns are gathered at the edge of the Dark Forest and Flameshooter is with them. They will be at your side at the first sign of trouble."

Danny grinned and raised his hand to salute the cricket. But there was no sign of Argill and no sign of the fairground either. Instead they found themselves standing in front of the drawbridge of an enormous castle. A river snaked behind it on its way down to the sea shimmering in the far distance. To his right, Danny could make out the shadowy mass of the Dark Forest and even thought he could see some white shapes moving indistinctly among the trees.

"I guess the adventure's beginning," Lucy said, glancing at him.

"Looks like it." Danny hoped he looked braver than he felt. "Here goes, then!"

They slowly began walking across the drawbridge.

The heavy, wooden drawbridge took them across a wide, deep moat filled with water from the river, which ran all around the outer wall of the castle as the first barrier against attacking enemies. Ahead of them, a solid iron portcullis set between two round towers barred their way. Black, narrow apertures in the tower walls gazed sightlessly at them with a forbidding air. There was no sign of people anywhere and the three friends found the eerie silence oppressive. Beyond the portcullis they could see a dusty courtyard and another guardhouse blocking the entrance to the castle.

Suddenly a trumpet rang out, making them jump. A face peeped out of one of the slits in the wall and then disappeared again. They watched as the portcullis slowly began to rise up, the well-oiled chains making hardly any noise. As they passed through the entrance several guards, heavily armed with swords and spears, glowered at them.

"Good morning," Tom said cheerily, but the guards just raised their weapons in reply. "Friendly chaps," he remarked to Danny, who smiled tensely.

"Ssh," Lucy whispered. "Let's not get into trouble right away!"

The courtyard was empty apart from the guards, who were lowering the portcullis back into position, and a jester who grinned at them impertinently, the bells on his hat ringing noisily as he jumped around.

"I guess that means we have to keep going forward," Danny said.

They crossed the courtyard quickly, feeling exposed in the open space. There were more guards at the second gate who again opened the portcullis and let them pass through.

The three friends gasped as the castle loomed in front of them. The impressive building dominated the whole inner courtyard, its many turrets standing proud against the sky. Its walls were made up of huge stones of every shade of grey and it seemed strong enough to withstand the most determined attack. A round tower stood at each corner of the castle, a green flag with a golden eagle embroidered on it flying from each pointed turret. The only entrance to the castle was a heavy wooden door, with two heavily armed guards standing before it. The walls were dotted with narrow slits where archers would stand if the castle was under attack and rain arrows down upon their enemies' heads. As they entered the courtyard Danny shivered, imagining armed soldiers positioned behind the thick walls, training their bows on them.

Walking forward, they were amazed to find themselves in a wide, open space which was a hive of activity. All of a sudden there was noise and confusion all around, and the ground underfoot was a mass of churned up earth mixed with straw and animal droppings. Various shops were set against the castle walls, some selling delicious things to eat, others wine and beer; an old woman sat in front of one shop, spinning wool on a spinning wheel. Carpenters proudly displayed their hand-crafted wares and candle makers had row upon row of candles on show.

Danny's attention was drawn to a forge in a corner, where a huge, sweaty man was busy shoeing a horse. Leaning against the wall were stacks of spears and lances, and there were many beautifully crafted swords hanging in a rack. They all gazed open-mouthed at the sights before them, turning to watch as customers bartered with the shopkeepers before finally making their purchases.

"What gorgeous dresses," Lucy said, as three women passed by. They were wearing beautiful, velvet dresses and heavy woollen capes wrapped around their shoulders, fastened with magnificent gold brooches.

"We do look a bit out of place." Tom looked down at his yellow and green trousers and pulled off his hat. "I feel a bit like the court jester," he explained sheepishly.

Danny laughed. "It would be nice to be dressed like them." Then he blinked and rubbed his eyes, staring at his friends.

Lucy was now wearing a long, red dress that complemented her copper hair perfectly, with a gold sash tied around her waist. A thin, gold band circled the top of her head and she had a pretty silk scarf around her neck. A black woollen cape covered her shoulders and she was wearing sturdy black, leather boots on her feet. She ran her hands over her dress, smiling happily. Tom, instead, was wearing a green tunic with a brown cloak and brown woollen hose. On his head was a simple hat and he wore heavy, pointed boots. Danny was wearing similar clothes, although his tunic was beige and his hose was green.

He whistled softly. "Phew! We really look the part now."

"Did you do that?" Lucy asked.

"I don't know, I don't think so," Danny answered.

"You must have done," Tom said. "It would be nice to have some weapons as well, how about it, Danny?"

Danny concentrated, but it was no use. No weapons appeared in their hands. "We could try and buy some," he suggested.

Tom looked doubtful. "I have a feeling our custom will be refused."

"Let's try anyway," Danny said.

Just as they began walking towards the forge, a large group of people talking animatedly crossed their path, pushing them to one side. A young man pointed to the castle, shouting, "Lord and Lady Grunden! Soon the feast will begin!"

A row of trumpeters dressed in green and gold livery and holding gleaming gold trumpets appeared on top of the castle ramparts. A glorious fanfare rang out across the courtyard and everyone stopped what they were doing and fell silent. As the last tones echoed around the castle walls and faded away, two tall figures clad in rich clothes appeared in the doorway. Danny craned his neck, trying to see over the heads of the people in front of him who were blocking his view.

A deep, pleasant-sounding voice rang out over the cobblestones.

"Lords and ladies, loyal subjects of my court, welcome to my dwelling. Please step inside and make your ways to the Great Hall, where a lavish banquet held in honour of our esteemed guest, Sir Daniel of Rootling, awaits you all."

A great cheer broke out among the crowd. Danny looked at his friends, the same puzzled look on all their faces. Lord and Lady Grunden raised their hands in a salute, and then disappeared back inside the castle, leaving the wooden doors wide open. The crowd began to make its way across the courtyard, everyone chattering excitedly about the upcoming entertainment.

"There'll be musicians and acrobats and even fire-eaters!" one girl exclaimed to her friends. "And later there is to be a jousting competition. They say that Sir Daniel is to compete against Sir Incubus... that is one event I don't want to miss." She walked away, still talking excitedly.

"Well, Danny, now we know when and how you're going to confront Incubus," Tom said.

"Jousting? I don't even know how to ride!" Danny stared glumly at his friends.

Lucy patted his hand. "Remember you can do anything here, Danny," she said. Danny tried to look more optimistic than he felt.

"At least we get to go to the feast," Tom said brightly, rubbing his stomach.

"Just remember to be on your guard," Danny warned.

"Do you still have the potion Argill gave you?" Lucy asked.

133

Danny patted his chest. "It's right here, Lucy. Why do you ask?"

"Maybe you should check out this Lord Grunden," she answered. "He may be Incubus in disguise.""I'll bear it in mind," Danny promised, his stomach churning at the thought of what lay ahead.

Chapter Ten
Inside The Castle

They followed the crowd across the courtyard until they came to the castle doors and made their way inside, their eyes taking a few seconds to adjust to the dimness after the bright sunshine outside. Flaming torches lined the walls, casting flickering shadows everywhere. Servants stood along the corridor, handing cups of steaming wine to people as they passed. Danny tasted his and found that it had a pleasant honey flavour that warmed him right through. They came to the entrance of the Great Hall, where jugglers and acrobats greeted them and musicians played loudly, accompanying a minstrel who was singing a ballad about an epic battle between two famous knights.

Long wooden tables and benches were placed all around the Hall, facing a raised dais at one end. A heavy oak table and finely carved chairs occupied most of the dais and a huge tapestry hung on the wall behind. Lord Grunden was sitting at the table, watching a nearby jester's antics with an amused look. He wore heavy, dark green clothes that gave him a regal appearance; a flowing cloak, embroidered with swirling, bizarre patterns in silver thread, lay casually flung around his shoulders.

Danny studied him closely, taking in his dark hair, slightly greying at the temples, and his arrogant Roman nose jutting over his neatly trimmed moustache and black pointed beard.

"Do you think that's Incubus?" he asked Tom and Lucy.

"Could be," the gnome replied. "Why don't you use Argill's potion and find out?"

"But if it's not him, I'll have wasted some."

"I think you should risk it," Lucy said. "At least we'd know for sure then."

Danny nodded. He pulled the metal flask out from under his tunic and removed the stopper, Tom and Lucy watching him encouragingly. None of them noticed the jester staring intently at Danny, a cruel smile on his lips. Danny let a drop of the potion fall on his tongue. It tasted of wild berries mixed with herbs and made his mouth tingle. He looked at Lord Grunden sitting at the high table. Danny waited a few seconds, but their host stayed exactly the same. Disappointed, Danny turned to his friends.

"He's not..." he began, and then stopped. He thought he had seen a dark form out of the corner of his eye. He looked again, confused, but all he could see was the jester entertaining a group of people.

"What's up?" Tom asked.

"Nothing. I thought I saw something over there, but it must have just been a shadow."

"You were saying?" Lucy asked.

"He's not Incubus. He didn't change when I looked at him."

"Well, at least we know now," Lucy said brightly.

Just then Lord Grunden turned his head and spotted Danny and his friends. He clapped his hands and stood up. A sword hung at his side, its jewel-encrusted hilt visible at the top of an ornate, silver sheath. He placed his hand on the pommel. Immediately the music stopped and everyone turned to face him. He stared at Danny briefly, his hypnotic, dark blue eyes like bottomless pools of water. Danny felt that he would drown in them if he looked for too long.

"Welcome, honoured guests," he said in his deep, sonorous voice. "Please find yourselves a table and be seated. Danny, Tom, and Lucy, will you do me the honour of dining here at my table tonight? My Lady will be joining us shortly."

He gestured towards the chairs at either side of him. Reluctantly they made their way to their host's table as Lady Grunden arrived. She took her place at Lord Grunden's side, staring with interest at Danny.

"It is good to see you again, *Sir* Daniel," she said with a malicious glint in her green eyes.

Daniel gasped. "Stregona! What are *you* doing here?"

"You didn't think I'd want to miss the joust, did you?" she replied with an evil sneer.

Danny went quiet, suddenly feeling utterly helpless. Lord Grunden looked curiously at them before he took Stregona's hand and sat down.

Everyone else in the Hall took their places on the wooden benches and there was a loud hubbub of excited conversation as servants began bringing in plates piled high with food. Enormous silver platters were placed before Lord Grunden, loaded with roast pheasants, quail, heavily spiced boiled meats, roast chicken and rabbit stew, and soon the table was groaning under the weight of all the food. A gasp went up as two servants arrived carrying the last tray, with a beautiful white swan sitting on top of it, so carefully prepared that it seemed as if it would take flight at any moment. They set it in front of Lord Grunden, bowed and withdrew. Another servant rushed forward and filled their goblets with red wine.

"Let the meal begin," Lord Grunden yelled, pulling a leg off a pheasant. He bit a huge chunk of meat and turned to Danny, Tom, and Lucy. "Please eat," he said with his mouth full, pushing a platter of quails before Tom.

The gnome picked one up and tasted it. "It's good, really good," he said, surprised.

Danny and Lucy helped themselves to some meat as well. Soon all the guests in the Hall were tucking into their food. Fire-eaters walked among the tables, shooting flames of fire over the diners' heads. The Hall was full of loud conversation and laughter, and also the occasional scream as a fire-eater blew his flame a little too close to a guest. The jugglers and acrobats also entertained the crowd, as plate after plate of food was carried to the tables.

There was every sort of roast meat; deer, hare, pheasant, beef, mutton and chicken were all brought in one after another. Several servants entered the Hall bowed down under the weight of a long plate with an entire wild boar on it.

Danny, Tom, and Lucy ate until they could eat no more, but drank little wine. Lord Grunden was a very pleasant host, telling them anecdotes about castle life and asking them all about themselves. Stregona merely picked at her food while watching them silently. After the roast meats came plates of freshwater fish, trout, salmon, pike and bream, all delicately prepared. Everyone tucked in eagerly, as if they were still famished. Danny and Lucy nibbled at their food, but Tom ate with great gusto.

"Isn't this great?" he enthused, his eyes shining brightly.

"I don't know how you can eat so much, Tom, it's disgusting," Lucy said, making a face.

"I like to see a man with a good appetite," Lord Grunden boomed. "Eat up, Tom, the sweets will be arriving soon!"

Danny and Lucy groaned. Now the servants were bringing huge cakes, caramelised fruits and steamed puddings. Lord Grunden leant forward and grabbed a handful of pear pie.

"Help yourselves," he said, pushing the pie towards Danny and Lucy. They each took a small piece and began eating it slowly.

"Have some, Tom," said their host.

Tom eyed the pie. "No thanks." He leaned back in his chair and patted his stomach. "I'm really full."

"Eat just a little," Lord Grunden insisted, a hard glint in his eye.

"No, really, I can't," Tom said. "It looks wonderful but I'll explode if I eat any more."

Stregona leant over and whispered something in Lord Grunden's ear, smiling slyly at Danny and his friends. Lord Grunden frowned, then nodded in agreement.

"Do you refuse my hospitality?" he said to Tom in a stern voice.

"No, I've eaten everything else," poor Tom said, confused. "I just can't manage the pie."

Lord Grunden stood up, an angry expression on his face. Two guards appeared next to him, their swords drawn. Silence fell in the Hall as the other guests realised that something was happening. He glared at Tom.

"This is your final chance," he said loudly. "Eat."

Tom looked at the pie and pulled off a small piece. He held it between his finger and thumb and slowly raised it to his mouth. "I'm sorry, I really can't eat it," he whispered. "I'll be sick if I do."

Lord Grunden smiled triumphantly. "Take him away," he said to the guards. They grabbed Tom roughly and dragged him out of the Hall. There was a moment's stunned silence and then everyone turned back to their food and began eating again. Lord Grunden sat back down and popped some almonds in his mouth. Stregona slowly ate some pie, smirking triumphantly at Danny and Lucy.

"Wh-where are they taking Tom?" Danny asked Lord Grunden.

"To the dungeons," he replied.

"The dungeons?" Danny and Lucy shouted.

"It is a crime to refuse my hospitality, especially when one is sat at my table as my honoured guest."

"But he ate everything else," Lucy said. "He was just too full to eat the pie."

"Then he should not have eaten so much before," Lord Grunden replied. "Now please, try these peaches in honey sauce, they're delicious."

Danny and Lucy ate in silence, wondering how they were going to rescue Tom.

The feast seemed never-ending. After they had tasted all sorts of different cakes, the servants brought out bowls of dried fruit and nuts which everyone devoured noisily. When Lord Grunden eventually declared himself full, the plates were cleared away and the musicians were ushered to the centre of the Hall. A great cheer rang out as they started to play and a minstrel began to sing. The guests banged their cups on the tables in time with the music and many sang along in loud, drunken voices.

"Is the music not to your liking?" Lord Grunden asked, noticing that Danny and Lucy were not joining in with the revelry.

"Oh no, it's lovely," they both replied hurriedly.

"It's just that I am so very tired," Lucy added, yawning widely.

"But where are my manners?" Lord Grunden beckoned to a jester standing nearby. "Take my guests to the housekeeper and tell her to show them to their rooms," he ordered. Then he turned to Danny. "Rest well, Sir Daniel, for later you will partake in our jousting tournament. My champion, Sir Incubus, is eager to compete against you."

"Er, thanks," Danny said. "Well, see you soon, then."

They followed the jester through the throng of people now dancing clumsily around the musicians. Once in the corridor, the jester turned to them.

"I can take you to the dungeons, so you can rescue your friend. In a couple of hours, Lord Grunden won't even remember he had him thrown in the dungeons, not after all the wine he has drunk today."

"I don't know," Danny began.

"Your friend will never be noticed among all the people that are arriving for the tournament," the jester said. "He will be quite safe." He started dancing down the corridor, the bell on his hat jingling merrily.

After a moment's hesitation, Danny and Lucy followed him. They passed enormous, decorative tapestries hanging on the walls and empty suits of armour standing eerily to attention at regular intervals. A wide flight of steps led to the upper floors, the white marble gleaming ghost-like in the flickering torchlight. Other, smaller passageways branched off from the main corridor, leading into the depths of the castle.

"It's like a maze," Lucy said.

"I know," Danny replied. "Just keep an eye on where that jester is going."

He was barely visible, skipping some way ahead of them from one side of the corridor to the other, his felt shoes making no noise on the stone floor. Danny and Lucy didn't dare call out to him to wait for fear of attracting a servant's attention, so they tried to follow him the best they could. But they didn't know the castle as well as he did and kept tripping on uneven flagstones and banging into walls as the corridor curved round.

"Bother," Lucy whispered as they rounded yet another corner. "Where's he gone?"

The jester had completely disappeared from view. They could see two passageways branching off to the left and right, and still others further ahead.

"Which way?" Danny asked.

Lucy shrugged her shoulders. "Let's keep going straight, maybe we'll see him around the next corner."

They carried on walking, hoping to see the jester at any moment, but instead they arrived in front of a large, open door at the end of the corridor. The room inside was brightly lit and a fierce heat came out from it. They peeped cautiously around the edge of the wall and saw that it was the kitchen. Huge iron pots and pans were hanging on hooks from the ceiling, along with freshly caught birds all waiting to be plucked for the following day's banquet. A roaring fire blazed in the enormous fireplace, where a young lad was slowly turning an ox on the spit. His face was red and flushed from the heat of the fire and he seemed half asleep. Several servants were washing the plates and cups that had been used during the banquet, while others were clearing away the remains of the food. People dashed about everywhere, all busy with their various tasks.

A big, cheery-looking woman stood at a wooden table in the middle of the kitchen, placing a plate piled high with enormous chunks of bread and meat onto a tray. Then she called over a young girl.

"'Ere, Sal, take this to the prisoner, an' be quick abou' it, there be work to do 'ere," she boomed. The girl took the plate and made her way across the kitchen.

Danny and Lucy quickly stepped back in the shadows, then followed the girl as she walked along the corridor. She turned off into one of the smaller passageways and made her way to where a tapestry was hanging on the wall. They watched as she pushed the tapestry to one side, revealing a door hidden behind it. She opened the door and went through.

"Let's hide until she comes back," Danny suggested. "We don't want to risk bumping into her. That door must lead to the dungeons."

They hid in a niche behind a suit of armour and waited. After ten minutes or so the girl reappeared, without the plate. She closed the door and carefully put the tapestry back in place. After the sound of her footsteps had faded away, Danny and Lucy went over to the tapestry and moved it, exposing the door. Danny opened it and they saw a flight of narrow steps leading downwards. A cold draught of wind hit their faces.

They followed the steps down, using their hands against the wall to guide them. It was very dim as there were few torches, and the further down they went the colder it became. The walls felt damp beneath their hands and the air smelt musty.

After what seemed like hours they finally reached the bottom. They found themselves in a large subterranean tunnel that stretched before them. Behind them a brick wall blocked the end of the tunnel. Danny took a burning torch down from its holder on the wall.

"I don't like the feel of this place," Lucy said quietly. "Keep an eye out for anything strange, Danny."

"Don't worry, I will," he replied.

They made their way along the tunnel, trying to make as little noise as possible. Their feet splashed in puddles of water on the stone floor, and every now and then a rat scurried away from them, its tail slithering along the ground. After a while, they came to a series of doors set in the walls on either side of the tunnel. Danny stopped in front of the first one. He could hear a groaning noise coming from behind it and the rattling, clanking sound of chains moving.

"These must be the dungeons," he whispered to Lucy. "Now we just have to find Tom."

"How?" she whispered back.

Danny knocked on the door. "Tom?" he called out in a low voice. The groaning stopped and there was a sudden sound of movement.

"Wha' ya wan'?" yelled a harsh, croaky voice. "Who's thar?"

Danny backed away from the door. "He's not in there," he said shakily and moved on to the next door. "You try the other side," he said to Lucy.

They went slowly along the tunnel, knocking on each door in turn. Unfamiliar voices responded, some begging to be let out, others calling them unpleasant names. Many of the prisoners began banging on the walls of their cells with their chains and soon the tunnel echoed with the noise.

"This is impossible," Lucy yelled above the racket.

"He's got to be here somewhere," Danny said. "We can't give up." Then they heard a voice calling out their names above the din.

"Over there," Danny shouted, and they ran to the door.

"Danny, Lucy," came Tom's voice. "Get me out of here!"

Danny tried the door, and to his surprise it opened. He and Lucy rushed in. There was Tom, chained to the wall, an empty plate on the ground next to him.

"Danny, thank goodness you're here. Get these chains off me," he cried.

Danny didn't move. He looked at Tom and then at the plate.

"Come on, Danny, help me with these chains," Tom repeated, more angrily this time. "What sort of rescue do you call this?"

"Danny?" Lucy said, frowning.

147

Danny shook his head. "Something's wrong. The door was unlocked... why?"

"I'm chained to the wall, I can't exactly get out," Tom shouted. "They probably didn't see the point of locking me in." He tugged at the chains to prove his point.

Danny still didn't move. "Hungry were you, Tom?" he asked, pointing to the plate.

"I was a little peckish, yes. What's wrong with that?"

"Only the fact that you were so full up that you couldn't even eat a tiny morsel of cake, which is why Lord Grunden had you brought down here," Lucy cried, beginning to understand. "Even you're not *that* greedy, Tom!"

Danny took out his flask, put a drop of the potion on his tongue, and looked at Tom. Slowly, Tom's face changed into that of a hideous ogre, with warts on its nose and chin and clumps of wiry hair sticking out of its ears. The ogre opened its mouth in a wide, toothless leer and rolled its eyes at Danny. Then its features turned back into those of Tom as the effects of the potion began to wear off.

"It's not Tom, it's an ogre" Danny said dejectedly.

"Welcome to the new Dreamland, Danny!" the ogre yelled, as Danny and Lucy backed out of the dungeon. They quickly closed the door, shutting out the noise of the ogre's angry shouting, and continued walking along the tunnel.

"This is hopeless," Lucy said, as yet another desperate prisoner called out that *he* was Tom and begged to be rescued.

148

Danny agreed. "We'll never find him. And the potion is almost finished."

Just then he noticed a movement further ahead. Holding his torch before him, he went to investigate. The jester's smiling face appeared in the torchlight.

"Ah, there you are," he cried out, relieved. "I've been waiting ages for you. Come, your friend's in here." He gestured to a door behind him.

Danny knocked on the door, calling Tom's name.

"Danny? Is that you?" Tom said from behind the door.

"Yes, Lucy and I are here to rescue you." Danny tried the door, but it was locked. He looked at the jester. "I don't suppose you have the key, do you?" he asked hopefully.

"No, but I do have this," the jester replied, handing Danny an old, rusty dagger. "Maybe you can force the lock with it."

"Thanks," Danny said, taking the dagger. After a few minutes of twisting and turning, the lock gave way. Danny flung open the door and Tom's beaming face appeared before him.

"Well done, Danny," he cried, flinging his arms around his friend's neck. "I thought I'd have to stay here forever!"

Danny pushed the gnome away from him. "How do I know it's you?" he asked suspiciously.

"What?" The gnome was speechless. "Danny, it's me. Tell him, Lucy."

"Prove it," Danny said.

"Sorry," Lucy apologised. "We need proof it's really you."

Tom stared at them both. "Proof?" he snorted. "Argill said to remember to trust each other at all times and that Incubus can't destroy our friendship unless we let him. It seems to me we're letting him."

Danny and Lucy looked at each other. "It's him," Lucy cried, and they both rushed over and hugged him tightly.

The jester coughed politely. "Excusing your graces, but anyone would have known that, seeing as we're all part of Danny's Dreamland," he said. "It doesn't prove anything."

"But it's me," Tom insisted. "Trust me, Danny."

"There's only one way to be certain," Lucy said, pointing at the flask around Danny's neck.

He opened it once more and shook it. "There's very little left, this could be the last drop," he said. "On the other hand, we have to be sure this is Tom."

He lifted the flask, then hesitated for a moment. Images flashed through his mind: the jester by the guard house as they passed through the outer wall, the jester by Lord Grunden's table at the beginning of the feast, the jester telling them to search the dungeons for Tom…

He raised the flask to his lips and finished the last drops of potion. He glanced at Tom and was relieved to see that the gnome's honest face remained the same. Then he wheeled around to face the jester. The man's brightly coloured clothes grew dimmer and changed shape until standing before Danny was a tall knight in black armour.

"Hello, Danny," he said in a deep voice. "I wondered how long it would take you to realize that the jester was me."

"It's him, Incubus!" Danny shouted to the others, but there was no need. They could all see him in his true form now. He towered over them, his armour made of a dull, black metal with a golden eagle etched on the breastplate. His hand rested on the finely wrought pommel of a long sword which hung at his side.

"If you want Danny, you'll have to fight me first," Tom said, standing in front of Danny.

"Not now, noble companion," Incubus said. "Danny and I will face each other very soon, at the tournament. I just wanted to introduce myself. You and I are very similar, Danny, we do not trust anyone, even those closest to us. I am sure we will become very good friends."

He laughed a deep, evil laugh and swept out of the dungeon, his footsteps echoing on the flagstones, then there was silence. Tom ran out of the cell, holding Danny's torch, but the tunnel was empty.

"It's OK, he's gone," he said, going back to his friends.

Danny's face was white and tense. "He's right. I don't trust anyone. He's going to win the tournament and Dreamland will be gone forever." He looked as if he was going to burst into tears at any moment.

"Then trust us, Danny," Lucy said, taking hold of his hands. "Trust us and we can help you save Dreamland."

Danny looked at both of his friends. "I–I don't know," he muttered. "I don't know if I can right now…"

Tom shrugged. "It's all right, we're here when you're ready." He clasped Danny's shoulder briefly, then they turned to leave the room.

They stepped into the tunnel and made their way back along the corridor to the flight of stairs. To their surprise, where there had previously been a brick wall at the end of the tunnel, there was now a wooden door. A bright white light glowed all around its outline. Suddenly Danny understood what he had to do.

"We have to go in there," he said to Tom and Lucy, reaching forward and opening the door. Brilliant white light poured out of the opening, blinding them. Blinking, they walked into a room bathed in light. As their eyes got used to the brightness, they saw that they were in a hospital room, and in the middle of it was a bed. Danny walked forward as if in a dream, with Lucy and Tom following close behind. Moving closer, they saw that a man was lying in the bed, beads of sweat on his emaciated face. His blond hair was greasy and unkempt and his grey eyes had lost their sparkle. Even so, Tom and Lucy could see his resemblance to Danny. He smiled weakly as he saw them approaching.

"Come here, Danny," he whispered, holding out a thin hand to the boy. "Give your dad a kiss."

Danny ran over and threw his arms around his father, covering his face with kisses. "Daddy," he cried, tears streaming down his cheeks.

"Gently, Danny," his dad said, wincing slightly.

Danny shifted his weight so as not to hurt him. "Sorry, Dad, I'm just so happy to see you."

"I know, son, and it's good to see you, too." He smiled at Danny.

"I–I want to say sorry," Danny stammered. "I didn't want to see you that last time, I was so scared, and then you never came home and I couldn't tell you why I didn't come to the hospital." The words tumbled quickly out of his mouth as if he was afraid he wouldn't be able to say them in time.

"It's OK, Danny," his dad said. "I understand. It wasn't easy for you to see me like this. Of course I forgive you." He hugged Danny tightly. "Talk about things, don't keep everything inside."

"It's too late," Danny replied miserably. "I've ruined everything. I have to fight Incubus in a jousting tournament to save Dreamland, but I don't even know how to ride a horse. I don't stand a chance."

"Why don't you ask the unicorns?" his dad suggested. "They will be able to teach you to ride."

"Of course!" Danny shouted. "Oh, thanks, Dad. And what about Flameshooter? What can he do?"

"You will be needing armour, a shield and a lance, which I think the dragon is bound to have among all that treasure in his lair."

Danny gave his father a last hug. "I can do this, can't I?"

"You know you can, Danny. Your friends can help you. There's strength in numbers, remember." His father began coughing. "Now go, Danny, go win your fight," he murmured.

The man in the bed faded away and Danny, Tom, and Lucy found themselves standing alone in the brightly lit hospital room. Danny turned to his friends.

"My dad died last year," he said quietly. "I didn't want to go and visit him in hospital because he frightened me, he looked so different. Then he died and I thought it was my fault, that if I'd gone I might have saved him. Instead I let him down, and he died. I never told Mum, I didn't want her to be angry with me."

"Oh, Danny," Lucy cried, "how could you possibly think it was your fault?"

"I guess I always knew deep down that he would have died anyway, he was so very ill," Danny replied. "But I should have been there for him."

"You were only nine years old," Tom said gently. "It must have been difficult enough for your mum, let alone a child. And I think he would have wanted you to remember him as he was when he was well, not as a sick and dying man in hospital."

Danny's eyes shone with tears. "I think you're right, Tom." He looked sad. "Argill said that Incubus comes from my subconscious. That's what he meant by saying that he will grow until he destroys me... he was talking about the guilt I've been feeling since Dad died!"

Lucy put her arm around his shoulders. "So stop feeling guilty!" she said. "You loved your father so much that you couldn't bear to see him suffering and that's no reason to punish yourself. Tom and I believe that you did what was best for yourself and that your parents, especially your dad, understood how you felt. If we are to save Dreamland, you must believe it too."

Danny took a deep breath. "I will *not* feel guilty any more," he said determinedly.

There was a sudden, loud cracking noise. They all watched in amazement as the room began to break up all around them, like a mirror shattering into a thousand pieces. The light around them shone so brightly that they were forced to close their eyes.

Chapter Eleven
The Tournament

When they opened them again, they were standing outdoors in broad daylight. Blinking, they saw that they were in a vast field outside the castle walls. A wooden fence circled a wide area of grass that had been cleared of shrubs and weeds. Brightly coloured tents were dotted about the field, but there was no sign of any people.

"This must be where the tournament will be held," Lucy said, looking about. "See, the spectators will stand behind that fence and Lord Grunden will sit over there." She pointed to a raised platform covered with silk awnings to protect the watchers from the sun. "And that must be where you'll joust against Incubus," she added, indicating the cleared area inside the fence.

"Now I just need to find a place where I can learn to ride and joust," Danny said.

"You could use that meadow over there," Tom suggested.

Danny looked to where Tom was pointing. "Those trees block everyone's view from the castle, so they shouldn't be able to see me falling off," he said, grinning.

When they arrived at the field, they were pleasantly surprised to see Argenta and Joey waiting for them. Joey was wearing a saddle and bridle and looking thoroughly fed up about it.

"Look at you!" Danny said, throwing his arms around Joey's neck. The unicorn tossed his head, making the reins jingle.

"The saddle's OK, but I refuse to wear the bit. I can't understand how horses can bear to have that horrible lump of metal in their mouths."

"Did you do this for me?" Danny asked.

"Of course," Joey replied. "I'm not wearing this harness for fun."

"Am I going to ride *you*?"

"Only while you're learning. I don't think I'll be allowed to carry you for the joust, they'd be scared I'd use my horn if your lance misses!"

"Pity," Danny laughed.

"Are you ready, Danny?" Argenta asked.

"As I'll ever be," he replied nervously.

"Not everyone gets to ride a unicorn, Danny," Lucy said, sounding a bit jealous.

"I know, and I consider it a great honour. It's just, well, you know…"

Argenta nodded sympathetically. "We will make a knight of you yet," she said in her silvery voice. "Shall we start?"

Tom gave Danny a leg-up onto Joey's back.

"Now, use your knees to grip the saddle and use the reins only to guide Joey, not to hang on to," Argenta instructed. Danny tried to do as she said, adjusting his position whenever she corrected him.

For what seemed like hours, Danny painfully learnt how to remain in the saddle while Joey trotted, cantered and finally galloped around the field. Eventually he was able to stay on as Joey thundered at breakneck speed down the field, coming to a juddering halt at the end. Argenta declared him ready to proceed to the next stage.

"What's that?" Danny asked, rubbing his bruised bottom.

"Now you must do the same thing again, only wearing your armour and carrying your shield and lance this time," she replied.

"Oh," Danny said. His whole body ached and he couldn't see how he was going to be able to wear a heavy suit of armour.

"Then you will have to learn the rules of jousting," she continued. "But first, we must get you your armour." She looked up at the sky. Danny followed her gaze and could just make out a dark speck, far away in the distance. It rapidly grew bigger and bigger until Danny could see who it was.

"Flameshooter!" he cried joyfully. The enormous dragon landed in the field, his green and gold scales glinting dazzlingly in the sunlight. He folded his long wings, bat-like, against his body.

158

"It is good to see you again, young Danny," he said in his deep, serious voice. "Or *Sir* Danny, as we should call you now." Danny blushed.

"How goes our knight's training?" Flameshooter asked Argenta.

"Very well," she replied. "Although I think his bruises will take some time to fade!" Everyone laughed, including Danny.

"I have brought you some gifts," Flameshooter said. He unclenched his front feet and a sack fell to the ground with a loud, metallic clang. Tom and Lucy picked it up and took it over to Danny.

Flameshooter explained what he had brought. "This suit of armour was made by King Marcus' best blacksmith, out of the finest metals in all the kingdom. You will find that it is much lighter and much stronger than most suits of armour and that it will not dent easily." Danny ran his hand over the highly polished metal and picked up the helmet. He could see his face clearly reflected in the silver.

"Try it on," Tom urged.

Danny placed the helmet over his head. It was indeed surprisingly light and he could see quite well through the grill over his eyes. He lifted the visor and grinned at the others.

"How do I look?"

"Put the rest of the armour on and we'll tell you," Lucy said. She and Tom helped Danny into the armour, while Flameshooter called out instructions.

"That piece you're holding is the breastplate... that's it, slide it over his head, carefully now. Put the gorget on next, that circular bit, it will protect his throat. That's the pauldron, it goes on his shoulders, to protect his chest. No, leave the gauntlets, you can put them on last." They worked slowly but steadily, listening as the dragon listed every piece of armour and described its purpose. Finally, they stood back and studied their handiwork. Everyone gazed in awed silence at the silver knight standing before them.

"Well, what do you think?" Danny asked in a muffled voice.

"You look like a true knight," Tom stated.

"Any unicorn would be proud to carry you on its back," Joey said, shaking his magnificent mane so that it fell in flowing waves onto his arched neck.

"And any dragon would fear to do battle with you," Flameshooter said gravely.

Danny removed the helmet, grinning broadly. "Well, at least I *look* the part!"

Tom picked up the shield and lance. The shield was decorated with a fierce-looking silver dragon on a light blue background. The dragon's eyes and forked tongue had been painted in a vibrant red colour, making it seem almost alive.

"Very impressive," he said, handing them to Danny. "Be careful, these are heavy."

Danny put his helmet back on and reached out clumsily to take hold of them, his hands feeling like lead weights inside the heavy, metal gauntlets he was wearing.

"Urgh," he grunted, almost dropping the weapons. "I'll need Grullo's help to lift these. Where is he? I thought he'd have come too."

"We decided it best not to bring him along," Argenta said. "Everyone would run away screaming when they saw him, and he would be terribly hurt."

Danny grinned at the thought of the offended giant trying to convince people he wouldn't harm them.

"Yes, you're probably right. OK, let's carry on." He stood panting, leaning on the lance.

"The tip of your lance is not intended to hurt your opponent, that is why it is blunt," Flameshooter explained. "Your shield will protect you from heavy blows."

"I have to carry both of these *and* try to knock Incubus off his horse?" Danny exclaimed. "I can hardly lift them!"

Now his training really began in earnest. Over and over again the unicorns made him gallop up and down the field with his lance in his right hand and his shield on his left arm. Flameshooter instructed him on how to hold the weapons and how to use them. Tom and Lucy made a dummy out of sacks stuffed with grass and leaves, putting a target on one side and a counterweight on the other, and then placing it on a stick so that Danny could practice charging at it.

"Oh, well done," Lucy cried as he managed to strike the dummy. Then "Ouch!" as the counterweight swung around and hit him squarely on his back, knocking him to the ground. Tom helped him up, giggling uncontrollably.

Slowly, his strikes became more and more precise, until even Flameshooter complimented his attempts.

"Now he's ready," he said to Argenta, who bowed her head in agreement.

Joey reared up, whinnying happily. "We've turned you into a real knight."

"Th-Thanks," Danny replied shakily. "Just stay still for a moment so I can dismount before I fall off."

Glad to be on the ground once more, he took off his helmet, his damp hair plastered to his head. The sun was high in the sky and the day was very hot.

"I don't suppose I can take this armour off for a while, can I?" he asked Flameshooter.

Before the dragon could reply, a fanfare of trumpets rang out across the fields.

"I think not," Flameshooter said gravely. "The joust is about to begin."

Danny's mouth was dry and he was finding it hard to swallow as they neared the jousting field. There were now hundreds of people milling about, jostling each other for prime position at the spectators' fence. People fell silent and nudged each other as he passed. Indeed, the group made quite an impressive sight with Danny in his gleaming armour flanked by the two majestic unicorns, and Tom and Lucy walking proudly behind them carrying his shield and lance.

Flameshooter had decided to remain behind in the meadow, concealed by the trees.

"There are too many knights around for my liking," he had said with a glint in his eye, "and I don't even feel particularly hungry today."

The large field had already been prepared for the joust. A five-foot high wooden fence ran almost all of the length of the field.

"The Lists are ready now, Danny," Argenta said. "See, the Tilt is in place." Noticing his puzzled expression, she explained. "The 'Lists' is the name for the field where you will joust and the 'Tilt' is that wooden fence running down the middle."

As the group entered the Lists, a cheer went up from the crowd. They walked the length of the Tilt until they reached the end, where a servant was waiting for them, holding the reins of a dapple-grey war horse. The horse was draped in a light-blue cotton cover with silver trim and its face was protected by a metal nose-plate. The servant handed Tom the reins, then disappeared into the crowd.

"This is it," Tom said to Danny, stroking the horse's neck. "How do you feel?"

Danny grimaced. "I just want to get it over with."

"Just remember the rules, Danny," Argenta said. "You must knock Incubus off his horse to win, but you mustn't hit his horse or strike him from behind."

Danny nodded. As Tom helped him mount his horse, a loud booing rose up from the crowd. All heads turned to the other end of the field, where a dark figure was entering the Lists. Incubus was riding a handsome, black stallion draped in a luxurious green cover with gold trim. On his arm was a green shield with the image of a golden eagle and he held his lance challengingly before him. An elegant sword hung on a belt around his waist.

"Don't let him get to you," Tom warned. "Remember, it's all show. And it doesn't seem as if the crowd is on his side anyway."

Lucy removed the silk scarf from her wrist and tied it around the end of Danny's lance. "It's for good luck," she said, smiling at him.

"Thanks," Danny replied, a little embarrassed.

A fanfare of trumpets announced the arrival of Lord Grunden and Stregona, who took their places on the covered platform. Stregona glanced over at Danny and smiled sweetly at him with a malicious glint in her green eyes. Lord Grunden raised his hand and the crowd fell silent. "Good people of the Emerald Castle, let the joust begin!" he cried.

Hundreds of people cheered and clapped as Danny and Incubus took their places at either end of the Tilt. The horses shifted nervously, shaking their heads and stamping their hooves impatiently. Danny snapped his visor shut and held on to his lance tightly. He could feel beads of moisture running down the sides of his face and wished he could wipe them away. His armour suddenly felt heavy and cumbersome and he began to panic.

"Deep breaths, Danny," came Tom's reassuring voice from behind. "Just imagine he's the dummy you practiced on earlier."

Danny's breathing slowed down and he began to concentrate. He could see his opponent through the

164

grill in his visor, and he gripped his shield and lance more determinedly. His horse began to strain against the reins, trying to break free and charge down the Lists. Danny held it back with difficulty, keeping an eye out for the signal to begin.

A Marshall stepped out in front of Lord Grunden's platform, a white flag held in his raised hand.

'Here we go,' Danny thought, adrenalin rushing through his body.

There was a moment's silence, and then the flag dropped. Danny's horse charged forward in an explosion of hooves thundering on the grass, covering the distance between the two knights in a matter of seconds. But for Danny, time seemed to slow right down. He shifted in the saddle, slightly off-balance, as his horse began its charge and then watched as Incubus came closer and closer. He aimed the lance at his opponent's chest, making sure that his shield was protecting his own chest. As the two horses approached each other, the roar of the crowd seemed to fade and Danny could only hear the thumping of his heart in his ears. Suddenly there was a tremendous jolt along his right arm as his lance hit its target. At the same time, Incubus's lance hit his shield.

Tom groaned as he saw Danny lurch in his saddle, the weight of his armour dragging him further down and making his horse stumble. With a superhuman effort, Danny managed to pull himself back into a sitting position and the crowd cheered madly. In the short time it took him to sort himself out, his opponent's horse had drawn level with him. Incubus turned in his saddle and saw that Danny was in trouble. He drew out his sword and swung it viciously at Danny's head. There was a sickening clang of metal on metal, and then Lucy screamed as Danny slowly slid from his horse's back and fell heavily on to the ground. The crowd booed noisily, but Incubus just threw back his visor and laughed.

"Foul!" Tom shouted angrily, running over to Danny, who was still lying motionless on the ground. The gnome lifted Danny's visor, peering anxiously at his friend. Danny groaned as sunlight hit his eyes in an explosion of pain.

"Wh-what happened?" he muttered, trying to sit up.

"That *backstabber* knocked you off from behind." Tom gently removed Danny's helmet.

"My head's still ringing," Danny groaned, getting clumsily to his feet.

"Flameshooter's armour saved you from a nasty bump," Tom said. "Look." He handed Danny the helmet, which didn't have the slightest scratch.

The Marshall came running over to them. "Are you all right to continue?" he asked Danny.

"Yes, I-I think so," Danny replied.

"Aren't you going to disqualify Incubus for that foul?" Tom demanded.

"Lord Grunden has decided that the joust must continue, if Sir Daniel is able," the Marshall said.

"That's a disgrace," Tom began, but the Marshall was already walking back to the platform.

"It doesn't matter, Tom," Danny said. "I'll be ready for his tricks next time."

166

Tom helped him remount his horse and he returned to his end of the field. Once again adrenalin raced through his body, this time accompanied by a dull throbbing in his head. He shifted his shield and gripped his lance tightly. His courage faltered slightly as he looked at Incubus at the other end of the field, and a wave of doubt crashed over him.

'I can't do this,' he thought to himself. 'Incubus is too strong, he won't let me stop thinking about Dad and how I let him down.' He turned sadly to look at his friends. Lucy blew him a kiss and Tom shook his fists in an encouraging salute, while Joey stamped his hooves impatiently.

Argenta walked over to him and rubbed her head against his shoulder. "Be strong, Danny," she whispered.

Danny breathed in her soft, sweet aroma and suddenly remembered what Lucy had said to him back at the dungeon: *"Stop feeling guilty! Tom and I believe that you did what was best for yourself and that your parents, especially your dad, understood how you felt. If we are to save Dreamland, you must believe that too."*

He sat up straight in his saddle, ready for the joust. The flag dropped and for the second time his horse galloped along the Tilt. He focused his mind on Incubus's breast plate, watching it grow bigger as he drew nearer, until it completely filled his view. To his amazement, his lance hit its target squarely and he watched as Incubus swayed to one side, desperately trying to regain his balance. Danny barely felt his opponent's lance hit his shield and his horse galloped on without faltering. He pulled on the reins, turning the animal so that he could see what was happening. Incubus's horse was still running, riderless, towards the end of the Lists. Incubus was getting up from the ground amid jeers and taunts from the crowd.

Danny returned to his friends, jubilant. "I did it!" he yelled, pulling off his helmet. Lucy and Tom were jumping up and down, cheering and clapping, and Joey reared up, neighing wildly.

"Good strike, Danny," he called as Danny approached.

"He didn't stand a chance," Lucy cried. "You knocked him so hard that he couldn't get back up in his saddle, then his horse stumbled and he went straight down!"

"I wish I could've seen it," Danny chuckled.

"It's not over yet, Danny," Argenta warned. "You have both fallen once, so it is a tie."

"Incubus cheated," Tom said angrily.

"Lord Grunden has listened to Stregona's poisonous counsel and decided otherwise, therefore it is a tie," Argenta stated. "The next joust will decide the winner."

"No pressure, then," Joey grinned. He moved closer to Danny, so close that his whiskers tickled Danny's ears, and whispered, "He will aim just above your shield next time and will move his own shield to protect his breastplate. You should…"

A fanfare of trumpets drowned out his voice as the Marshall walked out to the centre of the Lists once more. Danny put on his helmet and returned to his starting point. His body felt cold and clammy inside his armour even though he was sweating profusely. He watched as the Marshall raised his flag for the last time. Lucy's scarf, still tied to the lance, fluttered in the breeze, its loose ends brushing against his visor.

"Go kick Incubus's butt, Danny, for you and for Dreamland!" Tom shouted, jumping up and down and shaking his fists.

Danny cleared his mind of all thoughts as the flag fell. His horse lurched to the right as it took off, throwing him off-balance. For one horrible moment he thought he was going to fall but managed to pull himself upright again. He saw Incubus coming closer, his lance pointing straight at Danny's chest. He willed himself to keep calm, holding his shield in its usual position. 'This is for you, Dad,' he thought, gripping the lance determinedly.

As he drew level with Incubus, he swiftly raised his shield to cover his breastplate and lowered his lance slightly. Incubus's lance hit his shield with force, knocking all the breath out of his body. At the same time, his right arm shuddered from the force of his lance's blow against Incubus's armour and there was a splintering sound as the wooden shaft of his lance shattered. Gasping for breath, he held onto his horse with all his might, struggling to stay upright. The crowd was applauding wildly as his horse slowed down. When it stopped, Danny lifted his visor and slowly turned around.

Incubus was lying on the ground, immobile, ignored by all the people swarming onto the field in wild excitement. Tom, Lucy, Joey and Argenta were hurrying towards him, shouting in delight.

The Marshall pointed his flag at Danny. "The winner!" he exclaimed, yelling to make himself heard over the noise of the crowd.

Danny's friends finally reached him, breathless with excitement and happiness. They pulled him from his horse, hugging him tightly, and helped him remove his armour.

"You've won, you've won," Lucy cried, kissing him on the cheek. "You've saved Dreamland."

"All thanks to my friends," Danny laughed, relieved it was all over. He looked around happily at them all.

"Beware, Sir Daniel," came a cry. Danny looked up to see the Marshall waving his arms and pointing further down the field. Danny saw Stregona helping Incubus to his feet and stiffened as he watched his opponent start walking towards him with his sword drawn. Tom and Joey placed themselves in front of Danny to protect him. Then there was a swooshing noise as Flameshooter landed with a thump on the ground beside them. Everyone on the field stopped in their tracks, suddenly silent.

"Be gone, evil one," Flameshooter roared. "Danny has defeated you, now you must leave Dreamland. Those were the terms."

Incubus took another step forward. "I will claim my prize," he boomed. "Danny is mine."

"Danny beat you fair and square," Tom shouted. "He didn't need any tricks to do it, either!"

Incubus turned to Danny. "Dreamland is mine. I am a part of you, you created me and without me you are nothing."

"No!" Danny yelled. "You fed on my guilt over my dad. Well, let me tell you that I forgive myself for everything, it wasn't my fault."

"No!" Incubus stretched his hand out towards Danny, gripping his arm.

Danny stood firm. "I forgive myself!" he repeated.

The hand slipped from Danny's arm, then Incubus staggered back. For a moment, he stood there, swaying as if on a boat, then fell flat on his face. As the friends watched, the suit of armour disintegrated and they gasped when they realised it was empty.

"He's gone," Danny said, surprised. "It's over."

"No it's not," Joey cried. "Look!"

The crowd of people faded before their eyes and disappeared. Ivy began to grow over the castle walls, rapidly engulfing them. With a rumbling noise the castle towers collapsed, dust and debris rising up into the air. Within a few minutes ivy covered everything; the castle walls began to crumble and the group of friends found themselves gazing at a desolate ruin. The silence was deafening.

"Now it is over," Flameshooter said quietly.

The castle, the field and the brightly coloured tents faded away, leaving Danny and his friends surrounded by the grey mist. Then the fog cleared and the familiar sights and sounds of the fairground suddenly appeared. They found themselves standing by Tom's stall, surrounded by many smiling faces. Everyone was cheering loudly, chanting Danny's name over and over again.

"Well done, Danny," said a voice in his ear. Turning, Danny saw Argill standing next to him and grinned happily. The cricket raised his hand for silence.

"Today is an extraordinary day for Dreamland. Our friend Danny has vanquished Incubus through dogged determination, never doubting himself." He paused while everyone applauded.

Danny went red. "I only got through this thanks to my friends," he said loudly. "They believed in me and gave me the strength to win. Thanks, all of you." He gave each of them a hug, until they all had tears in their eyes.

"Does this mean you're coming back then?" Joey asked cheekily.

"You bet!" Danny exclaimed.

A table appeared laden with doughnuts, popcorn, hot dogs and fizzy drinks and soon a party was well under way. Danny looked around at all the happy, smiling faces and felt himself glowing warmly inside.

"You should feel proud of yourself, Danny," Argill said quietly to him. "We are all very grateful for what you have done for us."

"I couldn't let Incubus take over Dreamland," Danny replied.

"I know. However, Incubus was part of your subconscious. You have defeated him for now but he could return in the future, if you let him."

"I won't let him," Danny stated firmly.

"How will you do that?" Argill asked.

"By talking about my dad."

"There is someone in particular you should talk to, Danny," the cricket said, staring at him intently.

Danny thought for a moment, then suddenly understood. "You mean I should talk to my mum," he said.

"Will you?"

"Yes. I-I've wanted to talk to her for ages about Dad, but I was scared of upsetting her."

"It is always better to get these things out in the open," Argill said gravely.

"I know that now," Danny said. "I've got loads of things I want to ask her."

"Good luck, Danny, and we will see each other again soon," Argill said, walking slowly away.

Danny watched him go until he could no longer see him in the crowd, then turned to his friends with a huge smile on his face, and joined in with the festivities.

Danny kept his promise to Argill the following morning and spoke with his mum after he had eaten his breakfast. It took him a while to pluck up the courage to start talking, but once he did, the words just tumbled out one after another and he found that it wasn't as painful as he had expected. She listened in silence, waiting patiently until he had finished. Then she took him into her arms and the two of them hugged each other tightly, tears streaming down their faces.

Afterwards, they took a picnic to the tree house where they laughed and talked for hours. Danny listened, enraptured, as his mum told him funny anecdotes while they looked through a box of old photos. She picked one up and showed it to Danny, who burst out laughing at the sight of his parents' long hair and garish clothes.

"That was taken on our first date," his mum said, giggling. "Everyone looked like that in the late seventies, your dad and I were actually pretty hip back then. Just think, we were only eighteen years old when that photo was taken."

They spent such a wonderful afternoon together in the tree house that Danny wished it would never end.

"Let's do this again soon, Mum," he said as they went back indoors.

"Any time you want," she replied, hugging him.

That evening, when his mum went into Danny's room to say goodnight, she found him sat up in bed gazing thoughtfully at his Dreamland ticket.

"Who gave *you* the silver ticket?" Danny asked her as she sat down on the edge of his bed.

"Your aunty Lisa," she replied. "My mum, your nana, gave it to her and when Lisa didn't want it any more, she gave it to me. I used it for a long time, until I met your dad, actually. I used to love going to

174

Dreamland and having exciting adventures so much that I couldn't wait to go to sleep at night."

"Did you make any friends there?"

"Of course. There was a young boy called Ben and his older sister, Annie, who both met me every time I visited Dreamland. Then there were all the other people we met on our adventures… over the years we saw many of them again and again. And Argill the cricket kept an eye on things and helped us if we got into trouble, which was quite often!"

"Argill helped me, too," Danny said.

"Make sure you listen to him, Danny, he is a very wise cricket," she told him.

"I know," he replied. He hesitated, and then asked, "Did anything bad ever happen to you there?"

"Only once. I went into the Dark Forest, even though everyone told me not to, and almost got caught by Stregona. I only managed to escape thanks to a unicorn who rescued me."

"What was the unicorn's name?"

She thought for a moment. "I think it was Fastfoot… no, wait, it was Fleetfoot, I'm sure it was."

"Fleetfoot?" Danny exclaimed. "I helped rescue his son, Joey, on my first visit to Dreamland! I had to save him from Grullo the giant."

"Did something happen in Dreamland?" his mum asked curiously. "Is that why you decided to talk to me now about your dad?"

Danny sighed. "I accidentally let an evil character called Incubus into Dreamland. He tried to destroy everything and ruin our adventures and he almost succeeded, until my friends there helped me overcome him in a jousting tournament. After I defeated Incubus, Argill said I should talk to you, otherwise he could come back again."

"That sounds interesting," his mum said. "Tell me more."

So Danny told her all about his battle against Incubus, about Tom and Lucy and about the many other adventures he had had in Dreamland. She listened carefully, laughing as he described how he had solved the problem of Grullo the giant by giving him shiny sweet wrappers, then gasping in horror as he described his encounter with the sabre-toothed tiger. He told her how Stregona had tricked them by pretending to be a scared little girl, and how he had broken her spell over Flameshooter so that the dragon could help them escape.

"This is better than any book we've ever read together," she said, amazed.

After he had finished telling her everything, he gave a big yawn. "Gosh, I'm tired," he said.His mum gave him a hug and kissed him goodnight. "I'm looking forward to the next instalment," she smiled, ruffling his hair affectionately. She left the room and quietly closed the bedroom door. Danny picked up the book on his bedside table and looked at the cover. "Hmm, cowboys and indians," he murmured. "Could be interesting."

He turned off his bedroom light and placed the silver ticket under his pillow. He snuggled down underneath the covers, eager to have lots more exciting adventures with all his friends in Dreamland.

THE END

Glossary of Names

A few of the characters' names in Dreamland come from Italian, here are their meanings.

Argill comes from 'argilla', which means clay. Unlike in Italian, here it's pronounced with a hard 'g' sound, like the g in girl.

Stregona comes from 'strega', which means witch.

Argenta comes from 'argento', which means silver.

Lucinda comes from 'luce', which means light.

Grullo means silly or foolish in Tuscany, very appropriate for the giant!

Malia means a spell, or an enchantment, or sorcery.

Incubus comes from 'incubo', which means nightmare.

Grunden come from 'grun', which means green in German.

ACKNOWLEDGEMENTS

First of all, I would like to thank my wonderful readers, Francesco Valla, age 14, Jess Webb, age 12, Abigail Northwood, age 11, Bronwyn Northwood, age 8, Jack Pryke, age 8, and Alex Brown of RColourMusic, age 7, who took the time to read Dreamland and let me know what they thought of it. Their feedback was invaluable, and very much appreciated. You're all stars!

Thanks also to my beta readers Sarah N, April, Jo, Robin, Julia, Patrycja, Fiona, Krissy, John and Abigail. Thanks for all your help and support!

A special thank you goes to my son for his (almost) unlimited patience in helping me design and create the cover for Dreamland. Words cannot say what a help he has been.

And lastly, as usual, thank you to my husband, Ivan, who puts up with my temper tantrums, creative outbursts, and my forgetting to cook dinner! What would I do without you?!

Thank you for reading this story, I hope you enjoyed Danny's adventures in Dreamland.

You can contact me at:

facebook.com/juliaclementsauthor

twitter.com/JuliaEClements1

goodreads.com/author/show/17135908.Julia_ E_Clements

And maybe you could ask Mum or Dad to help you write a review on Amazon, so other kids can enjoy reading Dreamland too!

Dreamland is also available as an **audiobook**, read by the wonderful Kae Denino!

My latest book, **Adventure in Malasorte Castle**, is now available at all online retailers in paperback and ebook!
books2read.com/MalasorteCastle

And if you sign up to my newsletter, you'll also get an exclusive short story for free!
http://eepurl.com/dFC8p9